Lilura
Sl

"EVEN IF LOVE IS FULL OF THORNS, I'D
STILL EMBRACE IT
FOR I KNOW THAT IN BETWEEN THOSE
THORNS, THERE IS A
ROSE THAT'S WORTH ALL THE PAIN."

Naughty Or Nice

A Sweet Christmas Romance

Lilura Sloane

Lilura Sloane

Contents

Book Cover by [Lilura Sloane]

Illustrations by [Lilura Sloane]

[1] edition [2022]

Blurb

A fun romantic comedy, with plenty of steam!

Going home for Christmas is pure torture for Laney.

Being single is the worst thing she could do to her mother—it's not like she purposefully chose to spend an eternity alone, but have you seen the dating pool lately...

If she goes home for Christmas alone, she'll never hear the end of it.

She comes up with a genius plan!

If she can't have a boyfriend—she'd invent one, just for Christmas of course!

Poor Ethan gets signed up to be her new pretend boyfriend.

Everything is perfect!

Except Ethan doesn't show up...

But Beau does...

Laney hates Beau.

This Christmas is going to be a disaster!

Dedicated To You

This book is dedicated to you.

Yes, you reading this book.

To those waiting on love,

Be patient.

Love is a total drama queen.

It's just waiting to make an epic dramatic entrance.

One

A Strange Arrangement

"Please Ethan, I'm begging you, please." I hold my hands together in a praying motion while giving him my best puppy dog eyes, by the way he seemed to be wavering, my little trick seemed to be working, until I see him shake his head.

"No, Laney."

"Please, I will get on my hands and knees right here in front of all of these patients and beg you."

"You wouldn't dare."

With a sly grin on my face, "oh wouldn't I."

Walking round the receptionist desk, I couldn't believe I was doing this, but I really needed him to say yes, my life depended on it, yes I was been dramatic, but the holidays were coming up and certain things were expected of you, well at least if you was a

Powell, the very thought of visiting my family alone on Christmas Day was enough to give me the heebie jeebies.

"Why aren't you married Laney."

"Laney, why haven't you met a nice doctor yet."

"Laney, do you want to end up alone like your poor aunt Clarissa."

"Laney, you're too picky." The list went on, these were just a few of the things my mother said when she'd call me, she was worse in person, then she'd join the entire family into this tirade of why I was still single, I mean it was bad enough having to put up with being single without the moronic questions of why, "well, I don't know mother, maybe because the only men that are remotely interested in me, are slimy pigs who want to dip their wick for one night or want to fulfill their childish fantasy of bedding a nurse. I roll my eyes at the very thought.

Of course I never say this to her. I should. I should stand up for myself, but I don't. I shrink back and just allow them to steam roll me with all their comments on how I will end up as crazy old cat lady living with my flea infested cats because at twenty-six years old, I'm not getting any younger. I know it's unfair to ask Ethan to do this, but I really need him to help me out.

Kneeling down I instantly feel the hard floor dig into my knees, looking up at me he instantly bursts out laughing, "please, Ethan." I beg once more, shaking his head he looks down at me, his kind brown eyes instantly soften, "fine." He finally breathes out.

I want to jump up and down and do a happy dance, jump into his arms and tell him that he's my saviour, he literally just saved my ass from been steam rolled by the entire Powell family and I'm elated I don't have to face it alone.

"Never took you for the type who would get down on her knees, it's true what they say, miracles do happen." Glaring to the side of me I spot him. Beau Rivers the most brilliant doctor here, his crystalline blue eyes shine as he stares down at me, his dirty blonde hair falls over his eyes, tanned skin and the most muscular physique I'd ever laid my eyes on.

I'd swoon if he wasn't such a pig! Beau is the perfect package on paper, but the reality was, he fucked anything that walked and he treated women like he treated his sandwich, good to eat when you're hungry, but he never tried the same flavour twice!

"Jealous." I smirk, as I try to regain some self respect, I stand.

"Of what princess, I could have you whenever I want."

What an asshole!

"Oh please, Beau, your dicks probably about ready to drop off, if it hasn't already." I feel him lean in close, his shoulder touches mine—barely, "oh princess, my dick is just fine, I wonder how many nights you've fucked yourself thinking of my thick cock deep inside of you." Instantly my face burns, he usually does his egotistical banter, but never to this extent, my body instantly reacts to every word he whispers in my ear.

"Oh, stop teasing her Beau."

Once again he leans in close, "*who* said I was teasing." His tongue lightly grazes my ear as he says the last words and my body shakes in anticipation, I just stand there stiffly, not daring to move, not daring to look at him, with one sultry move, my body had defied me and reacted the way he knew it would react, but I didn't like Beau, I hated Beau, stupid female hormones! I think while staring into space.

"He's gone, Lane."

"What?" I blink rapidly as if in a trance.

"I said he's gone."

"Oh."

"Are you okay?" I shake my head, "I'm fine, Beau is an asshole."

"He's not that bad."

"Not that bad." I almost scream, but I don't want him to retract my invitation so I quickly try to calm down, even though I'm still shaking from the slight touch of his tongue, no, Laney don't think of his tongue.

"You know he's just teasing you."

"Why do you always stick up for him?"

"He's not the monster you paint him as, he's had it hard."

"He likes it hard more like." Ethan bursts out laughing, "Laney," he tries to scold but fits of giggles keep bubbling to the surface.

"Well, I better be going, can't stand talking to you all day."

"Charming."

"Why thank you, Miss Powell." He bows as if he's greeting royalty.

"Wait." I grab his arm before he can turn away to go do his rounds. "There is just one tiny detail I omitted to mention regarding Christmas."

"Oh, god." He groans.

"It's nothing major, just a tiny little detail."

"Just spit it out, Lane."

"You have to pretend to be my boyfriend."

"What! No way!"

"Come on, Ethan, please."

"Have you forgot I already have a wife."

"I said pretend, why are you being such a girl about it."

"I don't know Laney, it was bad enough going, but pretending to be your boyfriend."

"Please." I hold my hands together once more.

"Fine." He huffs, "but you owe me, big time."

"Love you." I blow kisses to him in the air, he shakes his head as he turns to continue his rounds, he's probably regretting agreeing to my ridiculous plan. I'd thought about ordering a boyfriend for the weekend, I know, ridiculous that you can order men as if you were ordering a Chinese, but apparently it was a thing. I wasn't that much of a lost cause that I'd order a man, maybe next year, but this year I'd have Ethan, whether he was happy about it or not.

The day went by pretty quickly and before I knew it my shift was over.

Ethan didn't stick around, probably scared there was another stipulation to my already idiotic plan, clocking out of the hospital I walk down the dimly lit street as night falls, wrapping my jacket tighter around my waist, winter had crept up, I could feel the biting cold snap against my skin almost painfully, stepping into Joe's convenience store I wonder down the aisle till I find the delicacy I've been looking forward to all day, picking up a tub of cookie dough I almost skip to the till, the highlight of my day is a tub of ice cream, and people thought us singletons lived the high life.

All I looked forward to was ice cream, Netflix and a lonely apartment, maybe I was doing this whole single thing wrong, but I wasn't joining a dating app, those things were terrifying, it was like closing your eyes and sticking your hand in the bees nest, you never knew when you'd get stung, no thanks! I'd rather stick to my boring, lonely mundane existence that I seemed to live, plus it wasn't all bad—at least I didn't have to share my ice cream, see, single life had it's good points too.

"Well if it isn't the answer to all my prayers." I hear his thick southern accent behind me, inwardly I groan, why me? Why can't I just grab my ice-cream and leave, why is he even here? Turning I greet him with my best fake smile I can manage to muster, "Beau."

"You know—." He leans in closer, "I wouldn't be opposed to you getting on your knees." I need a moment to recover, I don't understand why he purposefully torments me like this, to an outsider this would appear like flirting but he was just trying to get on my nerves and I had to give it to him because it was working.

"Thanks for the invitation Beau, but I think I will pass, maybe one of your disease ridden groupies would be better suited to that job."

Reaching his hand out he delicately places a dark strand of hair behind my ear, grazing my cheek as his fingertips move gently, a gasp tries to escape from my throat as shivers run down my back, "Now, Lane, why do you pretend that you hate me." He whispers.

I'd had enough of these games, he always had the upper hand, everyone knew who I was, Laney the coward who always shrunk back and never stood up for herself, I was such an easy target for people like Beau, I wasn't sure if it was the intense exhaustion that washed across my body or the annoyance that I wasn't dipping into my cookie dough just yet, but it seemed Laney had found a back bone. I had to applause my moment I wasn't sure it would happen twice. Moving closer, I see him flick a look of confusion, my body presses against his and I almost fucking melt, god! He feels so hard, no, Laney concentrate I scold myself. Placing my arms across his shoulders I play with the back of his silky smooth hair just allowing it to tickle the ends of my fingertips, bringing my head closer, letting my warm breath snap at his neck, I feel him shudder against me, "who said I was pretending." I whisper, flicking my tongue out and sliding it across his ear lobe, an instant gasp leaves his lips, "oh, fuck." I hear him breathe out.

Turning back around as quickly as I can, I dare not look at him, that was supposed to be a victory for me, but in teasing Beau, it appeared I had teased myself, no, I hate Beau, I remind myself, I can hear his shallow breathing behind me, "Hey, Joe." I smile at the kind elderly checkout clerk. Joe is a little sweetheart of a man, he's small with salt and pepper thinning hair, deep creases embedded into his skin, his small grey eyes look back at me and his warm smile instantly warms my heart, "well, if it isn't my favourite customer." He always says this, but he does make sure he's stocked up on cookie dough for the single spinster, so I can't complain. I pay for my cookie dough and bid him a farewell, just as I'm about to continue down the dimly lit cobbled stoned street, the door thrashes open and a strong arm pulls me back, okay, don't panic I think, turning my head, looking into those crystalline blue eyes, I finally take a breath, relieved that it isn't some serial killer lurking in the dark—it's so much more worse than that.

It's Beau.

"Seriously, what is your problem?"

"What was that in there?" His grip is still firmly wrapped around my slim wrist, I'd tell him to let go, but the warmth from his hand is somehow comforting.

"What?"

"Oh, don't play innocent with me Laney."

"Oh, the big bad Beau affected by little old me, never thought I'd see the day." I roll my eyes.

"Laney, I'm sure you know how to affect many men." I almost have to laugh at his slight comment, it almost appears as if it would be a compliment but why would he ruin the bad taste he often leaves in my mouth.

"Careful now, Beau, I might actually think your not as disgusting as I've previously thought." He pulls me tighter mashing my body hard against his, it's not like when I did it, he's that close he may as well have crawled inside of me, "now Laney, if you keep playing these games with me, I promise you'll lose." Pushing on his chest, I feel every curve of his toned chest and instantly my knees shake, a weakness overcomes my entire body, with a shaky voice I manage to muster, "who's playing."

He looks down at me, still holding me close, I hear him hum, his lips turn up into a small smirk, his head slowly moves towards mine. I can't move. I can't think. His lips are so close, I don't even think I'm breathing. I lick my lips, why are they dry all of a sudden? His smirk grows wider as his lips hit my ear once again, "when you lick that ice cream off of your spoon, close your eyes and imagine it's my tongue hitting your lips." This time he doesn't lick my ear, he gently takes my ear lobe between his teeth and tugs lightly while hitting his tongue against it, a loud erotic moan leaves my body and his breathing quickens.

"Hmm, it seems the elusive Laney isn't immune to my charms after all."

Why that jackass. I was sick of playing his stupid games, that's all this was—another game, was he that hard up he had to play these games with me, sure he'd have better luck with his groupies, who absolutely worshipped the ground he walked on, well I wasn't playing anymore.

"Go play your games with someone you've got a chance with."

"Laney—."

"Goodnight, doctor douche."

I didn't wait for a response, I squeezed out of his poor attempt at an embrace and turned and walked away from him, I'm not going to look back, I'm not going to look back I tell myself, but as I start walking away, my head slightly turns and he's just stood there watching me walk away, our eyes meet and he smiles, I'm not giving him the satisfaction of smiling back.

After all, I hate Beau Rivers.

Two

Cookie Dough

Storming into my apartment, once again Beau had left a bad taste in my mouth, slamming the door as I enter, I throw my cookie dough down hard on the side.

"Now, what did Ben and Jerry ever do to you?"

"Alisa?"

"The one and only."

"I thought you was working late?"

"It was dead, so they let me leave early, so?"

"It's nothing." I shake my head.

"Well, tell that to poor Ben and Jerry."

"I'm sure the cookie dough is fine." I mumble. "Well I don't know, I think he might need an operation." I burst out laughing, "For ice cream," I laugh even harder.

"Sure, so tell me, what crawled up your ass?"

"Beau, fucking Rivers." I groan.

"Oh, McDreamy."

"Urgh! Don't call him that!"

"Come on, Lane, that man is delicious."

"Yeah, deliciously—disgusting." I stick my tongue out, just in case she didn't get the memo that I found Beau repulsive.

"Will you two just fuck already."

"Alisa!" I scream.

"What? You could cut the sexual tension with a knife."

"That's not true." Shaking my head.

"Okay, you keep denying it but you two have been dancing this same old boring dance since university, five years down the line is a bit much don't you think?"

"We have not." I pout.

"What did he do this time?"

I retell the events of the day and she smirks at every disgusting moment I've been unfortunate to have with Beau this evening, her eyes widen when I recall the events that happened at Joe's convenience store.

"Laney—."

"Nope, I don't want to hear it, yes, I know you all think he's Mr. wonderful and I'm just mean—."

"Laney, we don't think your mean, just—a little oblivious to what's in front of you."

"What's in front of me is a man whore, who takes enjoyment at making me squirm every chance he gets, he's not mean to you like he is to me."

"Mean?" She shakes her head, "none of what you've said sounds mean, it actually sounds—well—hot."

"Well, you wasn't there."

"Come on, give the poor man a break—."

"I swear if you say he's had it hard."

"You of all people know he has."

"You sound just like Ethan."

"How is Ethan? I've not seen him for weeks."

"He's fine—he's my new boyfriend." I smile.

"You have a boyfriend?" She smirks. "What does Anne think of that, didn't know she was into sharing her husband." I laugh, "my pretend boyfriend."

"Oh, Laney, why don't you just tell them all to fuck off, a man is not the answer to any woman's prayers,"

"You don't know what it's like, if I show up alone, it'll be like I'm a teenager again, I can't stand the pity and the strange looks, the loud whispers and the constant taunting, it makes one weekend drag on forever, I just can't deal with the disappointment I know she'll have on her face."

"You'd think she'd be proud that you got your degree and you're in a stable job."

"She is but—."

"You need a man, hey I have an idea—." I look at her with curiosity, "walk in there with a smoking hot girl and over the hors d'oeuvre and champagne announce that you're a lesbian."

I just look at her with wide eyes, she couldn't be serious surely, my mother would have a heart attack! I could envision it now, she'd pull her bleeding heart out of her chest and before she'd take her last breath she'd say, "Laney, I'm disappointed in you." I shake my head, no, as funny as that would make an otherwise dull Christmas, I couldn't do that. They'd meet Ethan, fall in love with him and I'd get to spend a nice normal weekend with my family—well not sure normal is the right word, but at least I wouldn't feel like a leper.

"No, Alisa, I'm taking Ethan."

"Don't you think that's a little unfair to Ethan?"

"He agreed."

"You know he can't say no to you, you're like the little sister he never had."

"Well, what other choice do I have."

"I don't know, you could go with someone else—."

"Who?"

"Isn't it obvious?" I shake my head. "McDreamy." Is she joking? She has to be joking, it was bad enough I had to see him at the hospital because I didn't get taunted enough by my family, she wanted the torture to continue by been taunted by Beau, no thanks, think I'd rather go alone than have to put up with that.

"Beau? You want me to take Beau?" I almost scream.

"Sure."

"Have you lost your damn mind, I'm not taking Beau."

"It wouldn't be that bad."

"It would be my own version of hell."

"God! You're so dramatic."

"You don't know what it's like."

"So enlighten me, I never understood where this feud with Beau came from or even when it started."

"I—I just hate Beau, okay."

"Uh, huh, you keep telling yourself that, Lane." She sighs as she walks off towards her room.

"Come on cookie dough, you and I have a date." I talk into the air. Is it crazy to talk to your ice cream before you eat it? Well I don't think so, not like anyone else can witness my neurotic behaviour, grabbing a silver spoon, I settle down on the couch, popping the lid, I dig my spoon into the cookie dough, taking my first taste, I sigh with satisfaction, the yummy delicacy melts in my mouth, my tongue slivers out to catch the remaining dregs of ice cream that had stuck to the spoon and instantly I have a flash in my mind. Beau is in front of me, not a spoon and not ice cream, but Beau. I can feel his warmth as if he's in the room with me, except he's not, he only exists in my head, his tongue slides out running across my lips, sending electric bolts to rise up through my body, a small slip of a moan falls from my lips, slamming the tub of ice cream and spoon down on the small mahogany table, I sigh.

Thanks Jackass!

Beau had ruined my weekly ice cream ritual, his stupid words must have affected me more than I'd care to admit, now I couldn't enjoy Ben & Jerry without thinking of his stupid tongue.

My night was officially ruined! There it was—what had been missing since our accidental run-in.

The bad taste Beau always left in my mouth.

Three

Shadowing Rivers

The day started like any other day, sitting in the staff canteen with a steaming cup of black coffee, I wasn't a morning person, I actually hated getting up so early, so sitting here at 5am on a Saturday morning was my absolute idea of hell.

"So what happened." Although it wasn't all bad Alisa was on my shift this morning so at least I didn't have to trudge the day alone, I'd say she could join in on my misery, but she was a freak of nature, you know those people that rise early all refreshed with a smile on their face, yep, that was Alisa, I'm sure she came from another planet, it just wasn't natural to be that chirpy in the morning.

"What do you mean?" I finally ask after taking my first sip of caffeine, allowing the dark delicacy to slowly flow through my veins, hoping it would wake me up like some magic shot.

"I saw poor Ben & Jerry, and the poor bleeding thing had melted all over the table."

"Oh, shit."

"So?"

“Lets just say—I lost my appetite.”

“For cookie dough? Oh Joe won’t be happy.”

“Shut up.” I laugh while gently swatting her on the arm.

“Oh, don’t look now but McDreamy is heading this way.”

“Don’t call him that!” I grit.

“Who is he?” Beau asks.

“Nobody.” We both rush to reply in unison.

“Right, Powell your with me today.”

“Says who?”

“Cameron.” I groan.

“God, why does he hate me.”

“Laney—.”

“What, stuck with Beau all day, I couldn’t think of anything worse.” I’m expecting him to give me some smart remark back, but he just shakes his head at me and walks towards the other doctors.

“That was weird.”

“What?”

“Where was the smart ass answers I’m so used to.”

“I don’t know Laney, maybe he’s sick of you talking to him like shit.”

“Hey, you’re supposed to be on my side.”

“I’m not on anyone’s side, but this vendetta you have against him is getting boring, especially as you don’t even have a reason why you proclaim to hate him so much.”

“I do.”

“Which is?”

“I don’t want to talk about.”

"Fine, see you at lunch, I have to do my rounds." She stands, "oh, Laney, try be nice."

"I'm always nice."

"Not bitchy nice."

"Fine, but you're tying my hands." I hear a soft giggle, "you, Laney Powell, are impossible."

I wanted to tell her why I hated Beau Rivers so much, but she wouldn't understand, none of them would, while I sit blowing on my coffee, staring into space, I think back to that day that started my sudden dislike for Beau.

I met Beau when I was in university, all the women had swooned after him, not as much as they did now, but he definitely had a certain vibe, maybe it was his scent, everywhere he went they'd flock towards him like flies around shit, Beau wasn't interested though, he was dating Kelly Masters who was also training to be a doctor at the time, I sometimes wonder if that's what turned him into the disgusting pig he was today, back then he wasn't like that, he never entertained any of the women that would flock to his side, much to their annoyance. It was like a fairy-tale love that they shared, he told Ethan that he'd fallen for her the moment he'd laid eyes on her, that couldn't be true though could it? Sounded like something out of a story book.

Unfortunately their fate was not one that would last long, the reason they said he had it hard was because he had, he'd thought they were going to spend the rest of their lives together, it appeared Kelly had other ideas. One day she announced she was moving to Seattle, now this came as a big shock to Beau, but not as much as when she'd told him that there time together was nice but she thought he'd do better finding someone else, someone who wasn't going to be a million miles away, this crushed Beau. He'd spent many nights alone in his room, he wasn't eating, he wasn't sleeping, he didn't really come out of his room unless it was for course work, he started coming to the library, I spent every night in the library it was so serene and peaceful, it was like home from home, where else would I learn about nursing if not from books.

"Hey, Laney." First I was shocked he'd stepped foot in a library, then I was shocked he was out of his room, but what shocked me more was he knew my name and he was talking to me, he'd never really said more than two words to me since we had met and here he was in my domain making a conversation.

"Hey Beau, nice to see you." I was going to say 'nice to see you up and about' but given the circumstances I'd thought that maybe a little insensitive.

He'd come on a daily basis just to chat, I think he found comfort in our little talks and Beau was an interesting person, of course it also helped that he looked like he was molded in the image of a god! That man was fine, I didn't understand why he was wasting his time on me, but I'd grown to enjoy his company. I'd always know he was nearby, you could smell him before he even said anything, he smelt dark and seductive, like your favourite cup of coffee, deadly but inviting, his scent would surround you and you'd be lost—just in the moment, allowing him to cover you in his senses. I was starting to think maybe—just maybe there was something between us, something buried that was dying to claw itself out to reach the surface, my eyes lit up whenever he was around and I'd giggle and flirt like a love sick teenager, however I think the concept was lost on Beau, or if he ever had any inclination, he never made it obvious.

We went on a date once, it was perfect, how all dates are supposed to go, or what you'd envision a date should be like, the conversation flowed like we'd known each other all our lives, to an outsider that's what it probably looked like, he'd even walked me back like a proper gentleman, standing in the rain outside my dorm quarters I knew he wanted me to invite him up, but I didn't want to be just another notch on his bedpost, not that I'd seen him with another girl since Kelly, but I'd end up just been a rebound and I didn't want that. After all they never pick the girl they go with after the one that broke their heart and I couldn't be the unforgettable booty call that would start up every other booty call that would come, after all why would he put so much effort into getting to know me just to drop me after he got one night of passion—but I had to be sure, so standing in the rain I look into his mesmerizing bright blue eyes, getting lost in them, it was like looking into the clear blue ocean, his hand came around my face, pulling me closer, his face was that close I could feel him warm my skin with every breath he took, his lips every so gently touched mine, it was only for a moment, but it was as magical as I'd always thought it would be in my head.

I was waiting for him to take me in his arms, kiss me with an urgency that instilled passion into my soul and right when he'd push me deeper over the edge, my foot would pop, just like it did in those old black and white movies—but it never came, he just looked at me and smiled before he left, admittedly I was confused, he never said goodbye, he never set up a next date, I mean shit, he never even asked to come up, I wasn't going to say yes, but the fact he never asked confused me the most.

The next evening I went to the library as I always did, but his scent never attacked my senses like it had for the last six months, it was silent, he never showed. Walking down the aisle I hear giggling, but I need a certain book and each time I get closer, the giggling grows louder, that's when I see him, his arms are wrapped around a girl I haven't seen before, his lips brushed against her neck, her hands reach for his body, I should turn and leave, after all I don't need to see this, my cheeks grow red with anger? Embarrassment, I'm not sure which, I want to turn and walk in the other direction, but I really need that book, but he's got her pressed against the bookcase that the book I need currently resides on, so with my head held tall I walk right up to the gruesome twosome.

"Excuse me." They both look at me like I've just landed from outer space.

"Laney?"

"Could you just shift over, I really need that book." They scoot over and he finally lets go of her, placing my hands on the book that is the cause of my embarrassment, I pull it out, clinging it close to my chest, I turn and walk away as I hear their hushed whispers.

He swings me round to face him, "Laney, that's not what it looked like."

"No, what did it look like?"

"Well, what you saw—it's just." He runs his hands through his hair, I don't speak I just stare blankly at him, "you deserve someone good, I'm no good—."

"Please spare me the speech Beau, it was one date, it wasn't like the date you have going on right now—."

"You're special that's why."

"You know the only time a guy says that, is when he's coming up with an excuse to blow a girl off because he doesn't have the balls to say exactly what he means."

"But you are—."

"Goodbye, Beau."

"Wait, Laney I'd like to be friends."

"Yeah and I'd like to climb aboard a spaceship and fly to the moon, but we both know that's not going to happen." He just stood there gaping at me and for the first time since I'd arrived, I didn't stay and read my book, I walked away from Beau and took my book with me.

Over the years I'd watched him have a string of girls, they never lasted more than a day, some weeks he'd have a different one everyday, but I'd grown accustomed to seeing his extracurricular activities with these girls, after that day in the library things never were the same between me and Beau, once upon a time we were friends, but he'd ruined it the day he'd took our friendship further with that date and he'd completely destroyed it when I'd found him in that compromising position in the library, he could have took her anywhere, why would he take her there? But I knew the answer to that too, he wanted me to see him, he wanted me to catch him, because he didn't want to tell me he just wasn't that into me, so he'd done it in the most cruel way possible and I could never forgive him for that, that's the day I started hating Beau Rivers.

Four

Close Encounter

Walking to my doom, I imagined some horror music playing behind me in the background with each slow step I took towards Beau's office, yes I was being dramatic but been stuck with Beau for an entire day was my idea of hell.

The door was open when I eventually arrive, Beau was sat there at his desk, looking down as if he was overly enthralled in some paperwork he had laid on his desk, I grimaced as I glanced at him, "come in Laney and shut the door." I roll my eyes, so my appearance had been noticed after all. Slowly shutting the door I walk towards his desk and sit down at the empty chair across from him, he's gone back to ignoring my existence and I'm just sat in front of him waiting for his lord ship to speak.

"Oh, this is ridiculous." I huff.

"Is there something wrong?" He finally raises his eyes to meet mine.

"Why am I here?"

"I already told you—."

"Oh, so I'm here to help you do what? Fill the silence."

"Laney, why do you have to be a brat all the time, would it kill you to be civil to me once in awhile."

"Yes." He shakes his head as if I've disappointed him once again.

"So, I hear you have a boyfriend." He raises his eyes as a small smirk plays across his lips. Of course he'd heard about that, had he brought me here just to mock me, what an asshole. I didn't need this job that badly that I had to be mocked by Beau Rivers of all people, I'd had enough of his little games, he was like a little boy who didn't have the capacity to act like an adult.

"You know what Beau," I rise to a standing position, ready to make my grand exit, "go fuck yourself." Turning I storm towards the door, I feel a warm hand grip my wrist as he pushes me up against the door, my breathing instantly quickens.

"What's the plan now?" He quizzes me.

"Well—." A lump forms in my throat, I can't breathe, he's so damn close, that his familiar scent fills my senses, causing all sense to completely evaporate.

"You've just insulted me Laney, which is nothing unusual, all you do is insult me, what I can't understand is why, I've never done anything to you."

"No, you're fucking perfect, doctor douche."

"Laney—."

"The plan was to resign, if you must know." I say in a matter of factly attitude.

"Resign? You want to resign? But why?"

"I'd thought that was plainly obvious."

"Do you really hate me that much." His head comes close to mine, I feel his nose graze my cheek, instantly my body freezes, shivers course through my veins, can he feel my body trembling. I try push him away but as my hand connects with his chest, the searing heat of his body pulses beneath my hand and I'm suddenly shaking, his body presses even further against mine. I can hear his labored breathing in my ear as his hot breath hits against my skin, "Beau—." I breathe out, but nothing else comes out, I don't even know how I'm still breathing, he mashes his body further into mine, instantly my body stiffens as I feel his hard cock pulsing against my body, "do you not know what you do to me Laney." I hear his husky voice in my ear, "I find it hard to believe I do anything to you."

"Oh?" He raises a questionable eyebrow, he digs his body further into mine, now I can feel the throbbing against my thigh, the instant twinges between my legs make the heat travel through my body, my back digs further into the door. I'm not sure how I ended up in this position in the first place, I hate Beau Rivers I tell myself, but the pooling mess between my legs show me that my body clearly doesn't.

"Laney, you drive me crazy." I smirk, "No, Beau you're just—crazy."

"Laney—." He growls in my ear and my body goes into after-shock or some shit, before I know what's happening my hands are in his silky smooth hair, teasing the strands between my fingers, pulling his body even further into mine, the heat travels like hot lava to the crevice between my thighs, his head dips as he catches my bottom lip between his teeth, lacing his tongue gently across it, I stifle a moan, his lips catch mine, but it's not like that kiss we had on that date years ago, it's feverish, filled with passion and desire, gentle moans finally slip out into the depths of his mouth, breathless our lips part, "oh, Laney." I hear his gasp.

I couldn't do this with him again. I wasn't going through the same charade, he only wanted to finish what he had started years ago, he was trying to pull me in with his charms, and god damn him! It was working, I'd lost sense of practical thought, one moment and he'd pulled me into a sea of emotions, I couldn't do it again, so he could cruelly ghost me and tell me I was too good for him while he had his tongue down someone else's throat, no, I wasn't doing that again, this shouldn't have happened, but it had, one thing was for sure, it wouldn't be happening again.

I finally muster the strength to push him away from my body. I instantly feel cold, missing his warm touch against me, shit, five minutes in his presence and I was just like one of his groupie whores, begging for any attention from the dashing doctor, what was wrong with me? Hadn't I learned from the first incident with him, it might not be a rebound this time because Beau hadn't had a relationship I could recall since Kelly, no if you slept with Beau Rivers now, you were just another notch on the belt, I couldn't be a notch.

"That shouldn't have happened." I clearly state.

"Laney—."

"I can't do this with you again Beau, I told you before, go find someone you've got a chance with."

"What if I want you?" I almost laugh at his ridiculous comment.

"Come on Beau, you don't want anyone, women are merely playthings to you, somewhere to keep your dick warm for the night."

"Ouch, is that what you really think?"

"It doesn't really matter what I think."

"It matters to me, we used to be friends at one point."

"Beau, we were never friends and we were never anything more, we were never anything."

Beau's face fell flat, he wanted brutal honesty so that's what he'd got, we weren't ever friends, we'd danced close to being something but he'd ruined that after he'd cruelly rejected me and then we'd become enemies, nothing more than strangers, Beau was nothing more than a colleague that liked to tease me, nothing more, our relationship was purely professional, a little twisted but nothing more. He'd told me exactly what he'd expected back then, so it was only common courtesy I did the same for him right now, however I couldn't help the feeling of how his lips felt against mine, they still tingled from where he had touched me.

"Would you like me to go attend the first patient." He just nodded, I looked at him one last time before I left his office, it was strange, he seemed to be affected by what I'd said to him, but that couldn't be true, Beau didn't have feelings, the only feeling he had was when his dick got hard, he must be a great actor because he never even looked up at me as I turned and walked away.

Walking down the hall, I climb into the lift to go to the ward to meet the first patient of the day, the lift is empty for once, it's like the universe knew I needed to be alone with my thoughts, to collect myself after that—that kiss, god! No wonder women fell at his feet, I'd never understood it before until I found myself in a predicament with Beau, when he's near you, that close, it's like it's just you and him, he swims through your veins, enchanting you and the only thing you can see is him.

My body slumps against the wall of the elevator, I feel the cold steel at my back as I relive every erotic moment with Beau in his office, gently touching my lips with my fingertips, I can still feel them tingling from where his lips had pressed hard against mine. I shake my head hoping that the image of him will just fall out of my head, but all I can see are those bright blue eyes staring into mine, those plump inviting lips and husky voice that had my legs shaking and my body trembling, one moment with Beau and I'd completely surrendered to his touch.

Walking out of the elevator as I creep down the hallway, stopping just outside Mrs Greer's room, I make a mental note to never put myself in that predicament again, to never be alone with Beau again, there would not be a repeat performance of what happened in that room, all I had to do was get through this week and forget about Beau.

Simple.

Five

Memories

Sitting back at my desk I recall the moment I had with Laney, it was everything I'd been fantasizing about for years, every teasing moment had been worth the wait, she'd wanted it as much as I had but she'd spun a complete 160 and I was back to the person she hated the most, I just couldn't understand it.

Was it possible that she still harbored those ill feelings towards me because of what I'd done all them years ago.

I'd done that for her, didn't she understand that, I was a mess and she didn't want to get involved with me—not like that, I was doing her a favour, I'd thought by rejecting her, there would still be some semblance of a relationship, even if it was just friends, so I could keep her in my life, but that hadn't happened, she'd avoided me at every turn. I couldn't blame her, I'd rejected her in the worse way a person could, but what else could I have done, she'd have never understood why I couldn't be with her, what was I supposed to say, that I didn't want to ruin her because ultimately I would have done and where the hell did she get this groupie thing from, sure I flirted with women quite frequently, but I didn't bed them all.

Although I'd never corrected her because Laney had already decided long ago that I was a man whore who cared about nothing but my dick, for years I'd tried to get back in her good books and failed miserably, she was just so angry and aggressive and it seemed to be directed at me. I thought I could use today to patch what I'd broken, I hadn't meant to kiss her, that wasn't my plan, but every time I was near her, she just did something to me, I couldn't understand it, every part of her body screamed that she wanted me, however her mouth said something completely different.

She tasted like sunshine, she'd bathed me in light, in mere seconds of her lips touching mine, she'd allowed me to once again feel the sun on my face, that's what she was, she was a feeling of warmth you wanted to be near, she lit me up from the inside, her sly remarks were usually comical and I'd encouraged the behaviour by not saying anything, but what she said before she'd left my office was just cruel. Surely she couldn't have meant that, I knew our relationship was strained but I didn't want her to think of me that way.

I suppose it's no more than I deserved, there were less cruel ways to let her down, but I was young and stupid and honestly she'd crawled beneath my skin since day one and I hadn't known how to deal with it and now I was like the bad egg she wanted nowhere near her, I'd really fucked this one up, I just wanted a chance to redeem myself, to show her that her biased opinions of me were wrong but every time I'd get even a little bit close to her she'd run in the opposite direction, I just didn't know how to get back what I'd ruined and it was driving me fucking insane.

I'd tried over the years to just forget about Laney, she'd popped out of my life as fast as she'd popped in it and she didn't know it but she'd saved me from myself all those years ago, maybe that's what had scared me so much, that she'd seen all my broken pieces, the parts of myself that I hated most about myself and she'd accepted me—flaws and all, that was terrifying, that was the kind of girl that you never got over, if I'd have screwed things up with her, there would have been no coming back from it, so I did the only thing I knew how, I pushed her away.

The day I wandered to the library I'd gone there for quiet, I needed to stop the thoughts running through my head. I couldn't understand what I'd done wrong to Kelly, I'd thought she was happy, I'd thought we were happy and when she left, she'd left a gaping hole in my heart and in my life, I didn't think I'd ever recover and then I saw her, it was just a moment, but in that moment I was irrevocably blown away. There she'd sat at a table alone, in her own little bubble of paradise just reading a book, I'd never observed another person the way I'd observed her, but she was absolutely enchanting, I'd wanted her from that very moment, she hadn't even noticed me watching her. I'd watched her for days before I had the courage to approach her, she was always the same, dressed in faded blue jeans that clung to her slim frame, tight t-shirts that showed her ample curves and simple white sneakers, god! Even when she dressed down she looked like a sin I wanted to indulge in.

That feeling had never left, she gave me girl next door vibes but she was so much more, she thought herself as plain and unattractive to men. I mean the very thought was just preposterous, there was nothing plain about her, her bronze skin was silky smooth and her long chestnut hair was silky smooth, when she moved her head it would swish like one of the girls on a shampoo advert, she looked like sex on a fucking stick, there was definitely nothing plain about Laney. There was a hidden depth to her that I wanted to explore but I knew I couldn't because she bloody wouldn't let me, she was so concerned with 'my groupie whores' but what she didn't notice was that while she was looking at the women that would throw themselves at me, I was busy looking at her. She was the most infuriating woman I'd ever met and for someone so bright, she sure was oblivious to what was happening infront of her. I shake my head at the impossible woman that invaded my head on a daily basis.

Walking to Mrs Greer's room, I peek my head through the little square glass window and I see Laney sat beside her, smiling and chatting away, it was these moments that I cherished. Of course I knew as soon as I walked in there that there would be no smiles, no kind words, she wasn't unprofessional she'd put on a brave face, but that wall would be back up once I entered the room, the air would feel strained and clammy and my very existence would once again put her in a foul mood, so watching her from afar seeing her light up was the only time I got to see her like this, of course I'd hoped that she would light up when I was near her and those little fleeting moments when I'd touched her, being close to her, had my lips on her skin, she had, but it was short lived and she'd go back to hating the monster she thought I was.

Was I a monster? I didn't think so, but she sure painted me as one. Ethan had spoke lengthily of her distaste of me, he'd asked repeatedly what I'd done to cause her to act this way towards me, of course I had played dumb, acted like I didn't know, just chalked it down to teasing her, I don't think he bought it, but he never pushed for anymore information, there wasn't really much to tell anyway, I'm not quite sure myself, after all we'd only had one date, sure she probably felt like I'd led her on, hey maybe I had, but I hadn't done so on purpose. My feelings for her were real, I had wanted her, I still did, but back then I had a lot of growing up to do, they say men grow up slower than women—hey I don't make the rules—it's science, but I knew it wasn't any excuse. I would have apologized, but I couldn't bring myself to do it, I'd hoped she'd get over it, after all it couldn't have meant that much to her, but what did I know, give me a medical problem and I could solve it an hour, but give me a woman and I'd still be scratching my head wondering what the great big mystery was. Women, I had no idea how to solve, they were like pretty little puzzles that you'd never crack the code to but that was the great mystery, you weren't supposed to, although they expected you to know all the answers even though you, yourself knew that you'd never figure it out. Yes women were a puzzle and Laney was the biggest puzzle of all, trust me to want the most difficult woman brought into creation, well I wasn't a quitter and I definitely didn't want to quit on this puzzle, she thought I just wanted her for a quick fuck, but she'd got that wrong too.

I wanted to make her mine, to completely be enchanted by her, I didn't want her as a fuck, I just wanted her. I definitely didn't want all these 'groupie whores' as she called them, why were they groupies anyway, isn't that what rock stars had? She'd painted me with the same brush as an egotistical singer, I didn't know whether to be offended or amused, she sure was a funny girl.

She chatted to Mrs Greer's like they were old friends, but she had the same approach to all her patients, she had a kind heart and always made time for them, she didn't treat them like they were just another body that needed fixing, she treated them like people, like they mattered, her kind heart it was so attractive. She'd always had this way with people, she instantly made them comfortable and feel at ease, after all she'd done the same with me. I think it just came natural to her, I smiled as I watched her tending to our patient, her eyes look up and her gaze finds mine, shit, she'd caught me, that scowl instantly falls across her face and the once happy, lit up girl I'd watched moments ago is now gone and all that's left is the girl who can't stand me. I take a breath before I walk in the room with a bright smile on my face.

"How is the most beautiful girl in the world today?" They both look at me, I see a semblance of light flick across her face, then it's gone.

"Oh, you charmer." Mrs Greer's bashfully exclaims.

"Mrs Greer's how you feeling today?"

"I can't complain doc, oh and please call me Betty." She smiles.

Mrs Greer's had been brought in with a suspected heart attack six weeks ago, she had high blood pressure and diabetes, we were just keeping her in to make sure we'd caught all the issues going on with her, she was vibrant and cheeky for a woman of 65, but Laney seemed to love her, like she did all her patients.

"Laney, when are you going to marry the handsome doctor?" Laney's face instantly drops to the floor, that once rosy look has gone a nice sickly gray, she grimaces at the old ladies attempt at a joke.

"I think she's just teasing you." I whisper behind her, she jumps, her feet steps forwards then back, she loses her footing as she rocks on her feet almost crashing to the ground, my hands curve under her back as I catch her in my arms, she gazes up at me and she blushes—she fucking blushes, placing her back on the ground, she smoothes down her light blue tunic, "yes, well, um, water—your out of water, I will just go get some."

"Don't worry, dear—." She ignores Mrs Greer's attempt at explaining she didn't need any and rushes out of the room.

"Oh dear, was it something I said." Her little face wrinkles up with worry, walking towards her, I gently pat her hand, "of course not." I smile, "I will be right back." She just nods as I turn and leave the room.

I search the hallway for her but I can't see her anywhere, god, where could she have gone to now. Walking into the elevator I push the button to go down, right, she said she was off for water but as I walk into the cafeteria I'm met with silence, nobody is here, shaking my head I open the door to my office and there is the little flyaway bird sitting where she had sat earlier that morning but she was scrunched over with her hands in her head, quite strange that she would come here for safety when she knew I'd come in at some point and find her, did she want me to find her?

She looked so small, like a little doll, a doll who was sick of pretending to be strong, a little doll you just wanted to take care of. I knew that she knew I'd entered the room but she made no move to stand or even acknowledge I'd entered the room, she still sat there hunched over with her hands tangled in that beautiful mass of rich brown hair, walking slowly towards her, I gently place my hand upon her shoulder, once again she jumps. Standing up she's ready to bolt once more, catching her small hand in mine I spin her around, her body instantly crashes against mine, "please Beau—let me go." She pleads, she looks so small, I just want to take care of her, but then I remember she's not mine to take care of but right now I don't give a shit, so I pull her closer wrapping her in my embrace, her little heart shaped face raises as she looks into my eyes, "I can't do this with you anymore—I'm tired, it's exhausting, I just can't."

What can't she do? Hate me? Be near me? What does that even mean? I want to ask her, I really do, but instead I pull her tighter against my chest. I hear a sigh release from her body, this time it's not a sexual sigh, it almost sounds like a sigh of contentment, right now, this is the most precious moment I've had with Laney in years, of course I know it won't last, it never does, but in this moment right now, I close my eyes and take a mental image of her in my arms, allowing her sweet scent to envelope me. I know it won't last long, she'll come to her senses and go back to hating me once more, lifting a hand, I stroke her silky hair allowing her to melt into my body, once more she looks up at me, her eyes soften, but only for a moment.

"Why do you keep doing this to me?" She wails.

"Laney, I just—."

"No, it's not fair, I'm not sure what you get out of taunting me."

"I'm not trying to—."

"Yeah, well you do." She pushes her body away from mine and once again I feel empty, missing the touch of her warmth against me.

"But—."

"I have to get back to work."

"Laney, please—." She just shakes her head as she storms out of my office once more, inwardly I groan. I didn't seem to be able to do anything right, even when I thought I was doing something right, it appeared it was the wrong thing. I hated that she thought I was playing a trick on her, why couldn't she see that I was just trying to get close to her, taunting her, why would I? I just wanted her close to me, she smelt and felt like home and when she wasn't around it was cold, dark and lonely. I just wanted to make her feel better but it appeared I'd only made her feel worse. Slumping into my chair I groan, how had me comforting her turned into another argument, she'd seemed to enjoyed the comfort I'd given until once again she'd snapped back to reality and left, all she did was leave, maybe I should just face facts and let her, she'd not warmed to me in five years, I wasn't sure why I persisted in chasing a girl who couldn't wait to get away from me but as much as I tried I just couldn't stop.

Although she'd allowed me to comfort her, so maybe I was getting somewhere, of course I knew that was a lie, a lie I told myself so it made it okay to keep up the charade. I'd gave her space, I'd tried to be her friend, I'd tried everything but nothing had worked, each time I thought we'd took a step forward, she'd crush that dream and we'd soon be ten steps back. The feelings was clearly not one-sided which is why I tried so hard, shit, I'd never tried this hard for anything but I wanted Laney Powell and I was going to get her by any means necessary, she wanted me too, I knew she did.

She just didn't know that she wanted me.

She soon would, that delectable woman would be in my arms if it killed me. I may go insane before that happened but I'd happily end up as a mental patient if it meant I could put an end to this feud we seemed to have and finally I'd have her.

She'd enchanted me from day one, if I wasn't such a coward I'd already have the object of my desire, all I had was a prayer and a dream, a prayer that she'd forgive me and a dream that one day she'd be mine.

Right now, it seemed like a pipe dream, something impossible, out of my reach, but I did like a challenge, I think with a smirk on my face.

"Our story isn't over just yet." I say to myself in the cold empty space of my office.

Six

McDreamy

The week had dragged on for longer than what it should have done, however after that day of working with Beau, I hadn't seen him since that uncomfortable display we'd had in his office, the hospital wasn't that big, it was strange that we didn't cross paths for the rest of the week, not that I was complaining I tell myself, it was refreshing if not a little strange not having to put up with so much attention from doctor douche, huh, maybe I'd finally done it, maybe I'd finally pushed him that far I'd repulsed him. I grimace at the thought, not because I like Beau because I don't, I don't like him, just the playful banter helps to break up the day—yes I'm sure that's all it is, it's strange because it was like a daily ritual and when he'd disappeared, it felt like there was something missing, well there was—Beau.

"Hey, what's with the long face."

"I don't have a long face." I touch my face manically.

"It's an expression Laney." Alisa rolls her eyes.

"It's—it's nothing." She raises an eyebrow, "have you seen Beau lately?"

"Why, you missing him."

"Don't be ridiculous." I fling a scatter cushion at her, but it misses her by miles.

"He took leave for the holidays I think." She smirks.

"Oh, of course, the holidays."

"Speaking of holidays, are you coming to the Christmas party tomorrow?"

Oh crap! I'd completely forgot about that, the hospital throws a staff Christmas party every year, it usually gets worse than a frat party, college kids had nothing on us, I think while inwardly laughing, but if Beau wasn't attending this year I thought it wouldn't be so bad, after all Beau had been more flirtatious than usual lately which had me suspicious. I mean he generally teased and mocked me hoping to get a rise—which he usually did, that man just knew how to rub me up the wrong way! Lately it had been different, I'd not seen him with his string of groupie fans, I mean I get the whole doctor fantasy and all, and Beau was easy on the eyes but they flocked to him like fan girls would a celebrity, it never made sense to me, yes, this year I'd go because I'd be safe from Beau's charms, he'd left for the holidays, I had nothing to worry about.

"Sure, I will come." I smile.

"Oh yay." She jumps up and down, clapping her hands like a child with obvious excitement, I shake my head at her theatrical display, "what are you wearing?" I peer at her with obvious confusion, "come on Lane, you know it's fancy dress right?"

"I did not." I shake my head, "maybe I will just give it a miss this year."

"Oh no you don't, you agreed to come."

"It's not like I pinky swore, or even shook hands on it."

"Laney." She wails.

"Fine, if it gets you to shut up, I'll come."

"So, what are you wearing?"

"It's a surprise." I smirk. I watch as she goes for her late night shift, once again leaving me alone, I'm amused at myself because the great surprise of the costume I didn't know I had to wear was even a surprise to me, I didn't have a clue what I would wear to the Christmas party, something Christmassy I'd assume, it's not like they will all be dressed up as superhero's at a Christmas party surely—or maybe they would, who knows? Either way I'd just agreed so I had tomorrow to find a costume that I'd more than likely feel ridiculous in, thank god for alcohol, hopefully after a few beers I'd forget I was wearing the ridiculous ensemble—hopefully.

Getting comfy on the settee, I switch Netflix on, as **THE HOLIDAY** plays in the background, I grab the cream shawl that's draped across the settee and wrap it around my body, curling into a fetal position I allow my eyes to slowly close shut.

A loud rapping at the door breaks me from my peaceful slumber, throwing the throw off of my body, stumbling towards the door, I'm still in a daze as I open the door and there he's stood, in a crisp white shirt that can barely contain his muscular shoulders, rain dripping down his hair, little droplets running from his nose to his chest, tight black trousers that show every delicious bump and curve, his bright crystalline blue eyes gaze upon my sleepy eyes as I look at him with confusion, "Beau?" He simply smiles as he walks towards me, slowly backing away as he takes closer steps towards me, what was he doing here? Hadn't he started his holiday leave, surely he had better things to do than come here, his smile never leaves his face, his eyes have a dark hunger in them and all I can think is, *'oh shit, now I'm in trouble.'*

"Wh—Why are you here?" I shakily ask as my legs hit the settee causing my legs to shake and tumble, planting me firmly into a seated position.

"You look surprised to see me." He smiles.

"Of course I'm bloody surprised, you're in my apartment and you're not supposed to be here."

"I'm not supposed to be here?" He cocks an eyebrow, "well no not here, you're supposed to be on holiday, well yes I mean, definitely not here." I stutter, which seems to amuse him greatly, his rough hands come down on mine, pulling me back into a standing position, now he's close—too fucking close, "Beau, what do you want?" His hand curls round the small of my back pulling me closer into his body, "I'd have thought that was plainly obvious." I shake my head, because it's not, it's not obvious, it never is, I never know what's going on in that head of his.

"I want you." His deep whisper falls into my ear and I very nearly fucking melt!

"No, no you don't—you just think you do because—well because you haven't had it." Did that even make sense? It didn't sound like it made sense, why was I suddenly babbling nonsense like an idiot? I wasn't usually like this, even when he'd pushed me, which he'd done many times I'd never acted the way I was now, even those moments when I was weak and so close to giving into temptation, but right now I was babbling like some jittering little cheerleader who was elated that the football star was even remotely interested, no this definitely wasn't me, but I couldn't help it as I gazed into his eyes, I was lost, completely and utterly fucking lost.

His head comes closer to mine and I can't think, I want to look away, away from his deep gaze, but that's the thing, as much as I tell myself to look away, I just can't, I'm absolutely mesmerized just staring into the swirling pools of crystalline blue, I was swimming in his gaze like you'd swim in the ocean on a hot summers day, lost in his embrace, I never even noticed his head coming closer to mine, he catches my mouth with his, my head is swimming with desire. I should pull away but for once I don't want to, "god, you taste fucking sweet, I could kiss you forever." He whispers in my ear, "Beau—." But he's already undressing me with his lips pressed against my skin, every touch of his lips against my skin causes my body to shudder and tremble, and finally I let out a long slow moan that I feel like I've been holding in since we met.

His tongue slivers down, leaving a snail like liquid in its wake from his saliva, his hot tongue pierced my now cold erect nipple, I cry out, the pleasure swims straight to the crevice between my thighs, "fuck, you don't know how long I've been waiting for this," I hear his breathless whisper, he sucks aggressively causing my panties to dampen instantly, I'm so fucking needy I can barely control my actions, "please, Beau." I cry out, his hand dips into the cotton material of my panties, "fuck, your fucking dripping," the moans from his words fall out of my body like a banshee crying, finally I feel his fingers dip into my hot wet center, collapsing against his body and leaning into his touch as he massages the fuck out of my pussy, with each stroke, I scream inaudible words, bursts of pleasure hit my body like vibrations bouncing from the walls, holding on to him as I illicit a final release dripping all my pleasure onto his fingers, I finally do it, I smile, "god, your so fucking beautiful, I can't wait to fuck you and make you mine."

I hear an alarm, I'm confused, the light and dark dips in and out, the ringing gets louder and louder, opening my eyes, a sheen of mist covers them, blinking rapidly I look around the room and I'm alone—still laid in my fetal position on the settee with the shawl covering my body, my eyes search the room, but there's nobody here but me, did he leave? But as I look around I realise, he didn't leave because he was never here.

Shit.

Now I was dreaming about Beau, but it felt so real, looking down I see the slimy wetness coating my thighs, oh god! A wet dream at my age, how embarrassing.

But not just any wet dream—a wet dream about Beau, but I hate Beau, I tell myself for the millionth time today, why did I let him get inside my head, now I was allowing him to fuck me in my dreams, of course, I couldn't be mad at him for that, no, that was all me, but I couldn't sit around punishing myself for the naughty act I'd got up to in my dreams, I had a costume to buy, I think with a grimace.

"Laney will you just pick something, it feels like we've been here for hours."

"Well, I don't understand why we have to dress up."

"Well because it's fun." I roll my eyes at Alisa. "What's wrong with you today?"

"Nothing."

"I know that face, so spill."

"It's stupid and it doesn't mean anything."

"Great if it doesn't mean anything, then you won't mind sharing." I finger the costumes, placing my hand across each one, "Laney, if it's the costume—."

"It's not that."

"What is it then?" Turning I look at her with my most serious face, unsure how I can broach the topic without alerting her to some hidden mean.

"For arguments sake, say you have—." I lower my voice, "a sexy dream about someone."

"Like a celebrity?"

"Sure, or someone you really don't like, in fact you'd go so far to say you hated them."

"Oh-my-god!" She screams and I'm officially mortified, "You had a sexy dream about McDreamy."

Shit, how did she crack my code.

"It's not a big deal and also—don't call him that."

"It's a huge deal—so, was it good?"

"What?"

"You know." She raises her eyebrows, "It was phenomenal, but that's not the point."

"Oh?"

"Why now?"

"I don't know, you've seen a lot of each other and by what you've said there have been some very close encounters."

"There has not." I place my hands firmly on my hips.

"Why don't you just admit that you like him?"

"I don't like him, I hate him."

"Okay, girlfriend, you keep telling yourself that."

"But I don't."

"Sure, we all have dreams about been fucked by the person we hate the most," she rolls her eyes, "just find a costume and let's go."

Picking one up from the rack, I look over it, this might work, I think, after all it definitely fits in with the theme.

"It's cute." She whispers behind me.

"Yeah, I guess." Still holding it in my hands, walking to the checkout with Alisa, she's been quiet the entire time, she waits till we are in the parking lot before she breaks the silence.

"So you and McDreamy."

"Alisa." I wail as she just lets her laughter fill the air, I was quickly regretting even opening my mouth, I thought she'd have some pearls of wisdom to share, or at the very least tell me how to stop it from happening again, but no, she found my turmoil entirely amusing, thank god there would be alcohol tonight because I really needed to just forget about Beau, in and out of my head.

Seven

I Hate Christmas

The evening of the Christmas party had arrived and suddenly I felt a fluttering in the pit of my belly, why was I so nervous? We did this every year, probably not dressed like this though, usually I wore jeans and a t-shirt, I know not very Christmassy, but I had nobody to impress, so why not be comfortable, probably why I was single, the lack of effort that went into my appearance, but my life consisted of mostly working and sleeping, I didn't have time to date, nor did I have the energy to dress up like a fucking doll to appease the opposite sex, so that they could give me two pumps, a squirt and a see you later. So comfort was usually my domain, but not tonight, tonight I looked like Santa's little slut, I grimace as I look at my appearance in mirror, red and white striped knee socks, matte black Mary Jane shoes, which would more than likely render me unable to walk later on, that or I'd twist my ankle while drunk and face plant on the floor, a tight figure hugging ruby red dress that sat high on my thighs, a satin red choker around my neck with a bell, to alert everyone in the room at the ridiculous outfit and a little Santa hat that sat atop my chestnut curly hair, urgh! This was going to be a disaster I think as I look over my appearance.

"Oh doll, you look amazing." Alisa shrieks, great, I look like a fucking doll, another reason to hate this ridiculous ensemble.

"I'm not sure this is—appropriate."

"Why not?"

"Well look at me and—where is your costume?" I point at her outfit and she's wearing a glittering ruby dress, party dress I might add, not a ridiculous costume.

"Oh I left it at work, I will get changed there."

"Why would you leave it at work?"

"I didn't want to walk down the street and look ridiculous—." I eye ball her, she knows exactly what I'm thinking, "not that you look ridiculous—you look amazing—you always look amazing."

"Please—just stop talking." Her fingers come across her lips in a zipping motion.

"Alisa, I feel ridiculous."

"But you look—very festive."

"Oh yes, I look like Christmas threw up on me."

"Don't be silly." She laughs.

The walk to the hospital wasn't too horrifying, my only saving grace was that the dimly lit street was deserted and dark, the only thing you could hear were the passing traffic and of course the jingle of my neck with every step I took, it was like keeping track of a cat, was I the cat in this little scenario, well it appeared so. The only person who seemed to have an issue with my outfit was me, it's not that the outfit was hideous, in fact it was very flattering, but been in scrubs on a daily basis, these people I'd have to see everyday and they'd always remember the Christmas bomb I'd shown up in, plus it was more skin than I'd usually have on display, I wasn't one of those women that felt comfortable in her own skin, which was why I tended to hide my slim athletic frame. I guess I just didn't like the extra attention you'd get when you did show skin, it made me feel uncomfortable, I should have just wore what I felt comfortable in, why did I ever allow her to convince me to go to the party wearing this, I shake my head, I'm contemplating running back home to change, but we're almost there and all I can think is—at least there will be alcohol.

Stepping into the hospital was surreal to say the least, it was quiet as you'd expect, not a soul in sight. I'd put my bet on it that we were the last ones to arrive, which wasn't the best medicine, which meant only one thing—all eyes would be on us. Alisa still walked by my side to the large conference room where we held every party, it was strange, wasn't she supposed to be getting changed? Although did I really want to walk in there alone looking like a great eye-sore, no, no I didn't. I could see the colorful streamers adorning the ceiling as I peered through the frosted glass, everyone seemed to be on their way to being merry already, but you couldn't blame them, this would be the most fun they'd had before they'd have to be living zombies once again to care for their patients, well if they were already drunk, then they may not notice me, oh who was I kidding, I was going to stick out like a sore thumb.

Pushing open the two adjoining doors, the doors clattered as we walked through, way to make an entrance Laney, the masses of faces instantly turn, looking in our direction, just staring, it had to be the monstrous attire I had draped across my body, there were a mix of shocked and smirking faces, great, I just wanted a big hole to open into the ether and swallow me up, but of course I wasn't that lucky, looking at the many doctors and nurses my eyes scan the room, it's strange, nobody is in fancy dress, not one person, just me, my face instantly drops, how could she I seethed.

"Alisa, I'm going to kill you."

"Have to catch me first." She winks, while taking off at lightening speed and disappearing into the crowd.

Catch her first, well that shouldn't be hard. I'm not sure why she expected me to chase her in this ensemble, in these shoes, I'd break my neck, but she'd quickly rushed through the crowd in her black 7 inch louboutins at the speed of light, how did women walk in these monstrosities that passed for fashion, I really didn't know, give me some converse any day and I'd be happy, the faces still stared at me as I made my way into the crowd. I could see her dress in the crowd, rushing forward, I wasn't sure what I'd do when I caught her, but as I rush forward, my heel rocks, swaying to and fro, I was losing my balance, slamming into a hard body, his hands are at my waist, at least he'd caught me and saved me the embarrassment of falling flat on my face, probably with my bottom in the air because I hadn't embarrassed myself enough this evening, but luckily that nightmare hadn't arose because my hero had caught me, looking up so I can thank the man of the hour, my eyes widen and I inwardly groan.

"Well, Christmas did come early." He smiles.

"Beau—." But I can't say nothing more because all I can think about is the very sexy dream I had, his touch, his lips, the way my body melted against his, I could feel the burning as the heat crept slowly from my neck to my cheeks, shit, was it warm in here?

His head dips and that doesn't help the newfound pinkness that adorns my cheeks, "miss me." He whispers, I almost melt, why hasn't he put me down, we look ridiculous, but all I can think about is how close his plump lips are to mine and suddenly the flashback from my dream plays in my head as if on a loop, an instant gasp leaves my body, "you know Laney, you look like a gift I want to unwrap—with my teeth."

"Put me down, Beau."

"Are you sure," his hand lazily crawls up my thigh, shivers course through my body, with every light graze, my body trembles against his touch, "I wonder how wet you are little elf." His sultry voice whispers once more in my ear.

"Keep wondering." I glare at him, as I make a move to stand up and get his hands and lips away from me, I hear his deep hearty chuckle as his eyes never leave mine.

"I don't need to—that blush tells me everything I need to know." He points to my cheeks that are now burning, almost to the point of my own punishment.

"Asshole." I mutter as I turn and walk away from him.

Shaking my head, I wobble as I walk away into the crowd, but this time it's not because of the shoes I have on my feet, my body is still trembling from where he'd touched me, it felt like my legs were about to give way, if I didn't find a seat soon I'd have something else to worry about, the slick wetness between my thighs were a reminder of what he'd done, he'd barely even touched me and I was dripping for him, damn him, he'd known what effect he was having on me and still, he'd tormented me, I only came because I thought he wouldn't be here, instead Alisa had played a cruel trick. Beau had teased me as he always did and I'd had enough, I couldn't be bothered searching for my mischievous friend, after all I didn't even want to speak to her after the trick she'd pulled, no, what I wanted to do was to go home.

I was about to turn and head back the way I'd came, maybe stop into Joe's, grab some cookie dough and salvage the train wreck of the night. Stumbling through the crowd I finally find the bar, well, it couldn't hurt to stay for one beer I think as I grab a bottle of bud, allowing the alcohol to slowly slide down my throat, as the first taste hits my tongue I grimace, I always hated the first taste of alcohol, it lingered for far too long, bitter and disgusting, but after the second and third sip my taste buds caught up and it actually wasn't that bad, perching on a small stool, I look around the room at the happy faces as they dance, sing and pour alcohol down their own throats, yes, this isn't too bad I think, now that I'm alone and nobody is making me feel like the star of the show.

"See, not so bad." I turn my head and glare at my deceitful little friend.

"I'm still not talking to you."

"Come on, Lane."

"No, you tricked me."

"I wanted you to have fun."

"Oh yes and slutty Santa was the way to do it."

"You don't look slutty and Santa was a man—remember, you're more of a—."

"More of a what?"

"A sexy vixen."

"Nice try."

"At least you'll never forget it."

"No, neither will anyone else here either, why didn't you tell me Beau would be here?"

"I didn't know."

"I find that hard to believe."

"I swear, your boyfriend is here too." She winks, "Ethan?" She nods, "yep, coming right this way."

His arms come around my shoulders as he rests his chin on my shoulder,"hey, fake girlfriend." Turning round I swat him on the arm.

"Hey Ethan, no Anne today?"

"No, she had to fly out to Paris, some fashion dilemma."

"Oh, how the other half lives."

"So, about Christmas—." I wait patiently but a very drunk Dotty rushes over, almost colliding into both of us, "won't you dance with me?" Ethan side eyes me, "Sorry Lane, duty calls." Off he waltzes to dance with a very drunk receptionist, I watch as he spins her around the dance floor, her feet don't seem to be cooperating and if Ethan didn't have a firm grip of the young Dotty I'm sure she'd be on the floor.

I'm not sure how many beers I've poured down my throat but the swirling in my head tells me I've had more than enough, the pulsing pain in my feet also tells me that these shoes need removing so that I can feel the blood flowing through my feet once more. Standing I feel the pinch from the shoes and instantly I wince, half wishing I'd brought a change of clothes, but in my current state it was very doubtful that I'd have the capacity to change them. Stumbling through the sea of bodies proves a harder task than standing and trying to walk in shoes that seem to be trying to kill me. Every time I walk towards a body, they stop me with small talk and hugs like we won't see each other the following week, you'd have thought I was leaving for a year the way they were going on and not only a weekend, I've finally made it to the doors, crashing through them, I lose my footing and sway onto the wall, using it for support, yes definitely drunk I think while giggling to myself.

"Come on, let's get you home." Looking to the side of me there he is once more, "how is it, that you're always there right at the same moment I'm alone?"

"Call it luck."

"I prefer to call it stalking." I slur. "Call it what you want, I'm perfectly capable of walking home—alone."

"That, I very much doubt." He places his arm underneath mine and I jump at the sudden contact his gentle touch has against my bare skin, crashing back into the wall.

Clambering down the wall, I seat myself on the floor, shivers course through my body as the cold tiles hit my bare bottom causing my body to inadvertently shiver against the cool floor, my hands snake for the button at the side of my shoes as I kick them from my feet, a loud 'aaah,' illicits from my lips at the sudden release of having my feet trapped in a vice, holding my shoes close to my chest, I try to figure out how I can possibly stand now that I'm in such an awkward position, but I don't have to wonder for long, Beau brings his arms underneath my bottom lifting me high in the air, pulling my body into his chest.

"Wha—what are you doing." I sputter.

"I told you, I'm taking you home."

"And I told you—."

"Well, it looks like you don't have a choice."

"Still an arrogant asshole."

He never says anything as he walks with me in his arms out into the cold, night air, I clamber closer to his chest to feel the warmth radiating from his body, I can feel the vibrations from every step he takes, I can't understand why he doesn't just drive me home and he persists on walking with me in his arms, I know he wasn't drinking, so there's no reason for him to carry me all the way home, but as my head falls onto his shoulder and I find comfort buried close to his body, I no longer care, I don't even know we've arrived until I hear him calling my name.

"Laney." My eyes flick open.

"I need you to open the door."

"Why?"

"God, you're impossible, so I can put you safely in your apartment."

"I'm not sure if I want him to put me down, it feels so comforting and warm, it feels—no he needs to put me down, it feels a lot like my dream except I was on the other side of the door and I wasn't drunk.

With shaky hands I managed to fish my keys from the pocket in my dress, thumbling, I finally unlock the door, he turns the handle and gently kicks the door open with his feet, "you know I could have walked in, right?"

"I'm not sure you could." He smirks.

"All your fantasies must be coming true." He raises an eyebrow as he walks across the wooden floors and places me gently on the settee, covering me with the shawl, "oh?" I smile, "you could do every dirty little fantasy you've ever had, unless it was all just a rouse to tease me."

He bends down, nudging my body across so he can sit close, his head comes down towards mine and I hold my breath, his breath doesn't smell stale and disgusting like mine probably does, it smells of peppermints, I hold my breath, this is it I think, he's going to finish what he started earlier.

"Not like this, Laney, when I fuck you, you'll remember it."

"I knew it, just a tease."

"Oh, I haven't even begun to tease you, little elf." His lips press softly against my forehead as my eyes shutter close, I faintly hear the sound of a door closing as I slip into a drunken induced coma.

Eight

The Day After The Night Before

As the fresh morning light hits my eyes, I feel a throbbing in my head, like a pulsing heartbeat, I groan at the sudden rush of pain that pierces my skull, I wish I could forget the evening, but I remembered everything, the ridiculous outfit, Beau, yes I remembered Beau, he'd looked after me, brought me home, he was almost a gentleman—okay he was very chivalrous, not the ogre I'd painted him as after all, he was still an asshole though.

Ordering a greasy fry-up through **just-eat**, an amazing app that you could order food from every restaurant in the area, if you were too lazy to cook, or if you were like me and you were heavily suffering from a night of drinking, yes, that would sort me out and Betty made the best breakfast around town, if I wasn't in so much agony I'd walk to the quaint little cafe on the corner, it was like stepping into the 1930's, it was so calm and serene, Betty and her family always made you feel welcome, like the soft, kind granny I never had, no my granny was up her own ass, she'd pumped that much Botox into her face, she looked as young as I did, she wasn't plump with rosy cheeks and a friendly smile like Betty, she was always in the latest designer wear attending functions and bumping heads with the high society, I wasn't sure how she faked a greeting to all the people she secretly didn't like, I'd say smiled but that woman hadn't smiled in years, too many wrinkles you see, smiles were the devil to Delia Powell, unfortunately her snobby ways had rubbed off on my mother, I'm not sure why I wasn't like my family, but I sure was glad.

Demolishing my breakfast was an easy feat, isn't it strange, you wait so long for your food to be cooked and in mere moments every little morsel is demolished. I felt a little more human at least but I still couldn't help the nagging feeling of Beau's last words before he'd left, he didn't seem to know how to give up, but I couldn't think about Beau, not now, after all I had a nightmare to pack for, most people enjoy joining their family for the holidays, but not me, it was like walking into Disney world and stepping on a vortex that would open up and turn it into an 80's cheesy slasher movie. I'd like to say that my family were warm and welcoming but all they seemed to care about were appearances, sizing up each of the guests, always in competition, who had the better job, made the most money, who's dick was the hardest, it was a cringe fest! I couldn't wait for the entire ordeal to be over with, at least I'd have Ethan by my side to help me get through the nightmare that was fast approaching. Beau was probably going to have a perfect holiday with his perfect family, what I'd give to have a family like his, but no, I was blessed with a dysfunctional part of the high society.

Ethan often thought that I exaggerated about my dysfunctional family, little did he know I was being kind the way I'd portrayed them, but he'd see for himself, the shit show that was about to unfold, it still felt like punishment taking him home for Christmas, after all just because I had to deal with it didn't mean I had to punish others by letting them into the disastrous fold, but what choice did I have, bringing a plus one would take all the heat off of me and I'd had enough torment from the Powell family to last me a lifetime. Although it did strike me as strange that he wouldn't be spending Christmas with his wife, that's the whole point of having a partner isn't it? To share those magical celebrations and make memories, maybe I was a secret romantic but if I had a partner I'd be spending it with them, not attending a pompous weekend with the pretentious rich and cringey.

My family we're fine in small doses, after all I was the black sheep of the family, the one who brought shame down on their perfect image of what the family represented, what had I achieved? In there eyes—absolutely nothing, I'd achieved nothing. I was just a nurse who lived in a dingy apartment with a roommate, my mother didn't understand why I'd want to surround myself with sick people all the time, she said it made no sense, that's what the help was for. I roll my eyes at her biased opinion, you see in their world people in my field were beneath them, nothing but little worker bees that served their purpose in society, it didn't matter that should she one day need a medical professional, it would be that 'worker bee' that could ultimately save her life, no, that didn't matter, there was no place for it in the Powell name, but what disappointed her even more was not just the fact I'd gone into a field she oddly found repulsive, but that I was still single, perish the thought of having no man because in her eyes it was all about appearances and heaven forbid you be an independent woman in the 21st century—no man equaled failure. I'm unsure where she got her kooky ideas, but the disappointment laid heavily on me as I packed my remaining items into my suitcase.

"Hey doll, forgive me yet?" Alisa pokes her head in my room with a bright smile on her face, well who could stay mad at a face like that I think as I see her auburn curly hair bouncing across her shoulders, her deep set blue eyes glisten as she looks at me with her puppy dog stare, cute little freckles adorn her nose and a wide smile that would melt even the iciest of hearts.

"Already forgotten." I smile. She rushes forward wrapping her arms around my waist and nestling her head into my neck, "what was that for?"

"I guess I'm going to miss your drama."

"Very funny." I gently push her out of the embrace.

"How did you get home anyway?" She asks with a wink.

"Walked."

"Oh really?" I nod. "Well news on the grapevine was a very sexy doctor picked you up and carried you—I mean—how romantic." She swoons.

"Well if you already knew—why did you ask." I groan.

"Would you have told me otherwise."

"There's nothing to tell."

"Come on—that's romantic."

"If you say so."

"So?" She eyes me with a glint in her eye.

"So—what?"

"McDreamy carried you home, I want details."

"Will you not call him that, and there's really nothing to tell."

"Nothing?"

"Nope, he brought me home and left."

"Oh."

"You don't need to look so disappointed."

"I just thought—."

"What?"

"It had finally happened." I roll my eyes at her.

"Well keep hoping—it's never going to happen."

She giggles while flinging her arms around me once more, "you're impossible, have a nice weekend."

"Yeah, right."

I watch as she leaves wondering what she'd be getting up to while I was sitting in hell, of course it didn't matter because anyone's Christmas would suck a lot less than mine, but it was only one weekend I tell myself, I'm sure I can get through one weekend, I mean what's the worst that could happen? They'd sacrifice me for being single, okay, now I really was being ridiculous, anyone who listened to my woes about my family often thought I was just being dramatic, but coming from a wealthy family wasn't all it was cracked to be, think I'd have rather lived in poverty and had a family that actually cared about important things, like starving children in Africa, finding a cure for disease and famine, but no, my family's greatest worry was what they'd wear that day or who was on the hot list, it was almost laughable how plastic they all were. I'd often wanted to scream, that there was a whole world out there with real problems, but of course I'd just be met with strange looks of confusion, they'd probably have me committed for even daring to challenge their egotistical personalities, no it was best to just sit there looking pretty and pretend that I understood their dilemma of the month.

I hadn't heard from Ethan, so I was praying our arrangement was still on, he'd wanted to tell me something, but had been whisked away by a very drunk receptionist, I bet she was suffering today. I had messaged him earlier in the day to see if he was ready to meet the demonic clan but he'd not answered, I'm sure if he wasn't coming he'd have let me know. I was hoping he was coming, I couldn't face another Christmas alone with the spawn of Satan. I'm sure I was just overthinking the entire situation, that's because I'd have rather sat alone than gone anywhere near home for Christmas, as an adult you'd think I'd have learnt how to say no, but I just didn't have the heart to tell my mother that I didn't want to go because I'd have to fake enjoyment at being in there company for an entire weekend, but I wasn't like them, I wasn't snobby and I didn't care about high fashion or mixing with the rich to aid in my social status. I liked living a simple life and I couldn't fake anything,

I still wasn't sure how I was going to fake an entire relationship, but it couldn't be that hard could it?

The text I'd been waiting for had finally come, but it wasn't a text I was expecting.

Ethan

I can't pick you up, can you make your own way there, I will meet you there, looking forward to all the fun, fake girlfriend x

Great! Now I'd have to get a train and a taxi to get me to hell, but at least he was still coming, fun? Was he joking? Was that a lame attempt at a joke, there would be nothing fun about this weekend, but I was all packed and I had my fake boyfriend meeting me there, which wasn't part of the plan, but honestly I didn't really care as long as he showed up. Maybe that's what Ethan had tried to tell me last night, that he couldn't take me but that he was still going, yes that must be it. I hated traveling, the ride in his car was supposed to soothe me and get me ready for the nightmare, now I'd have to trudge halfway across the country to **Silver Lake Manor**—alone, yes even there estate sounded pretentious, it was named **Silver Lake Manor** because of course it looked across a lake that when the moon hit, it gave a silver glow, it actually looked beautiful in the moonlight, it was always my favourite place to go as a child, they'd search for hours looking for me when I'd grow tiresome of their lavish boring balls that they held in the ballroom. I'd often sneak out to the lake that was nestled behind the thousand acre woods, I'd never liked the manor, it was more of a show home, but the woods and the lake always made me feel at home, it was one feature that I'd always loved about the manor and probably the only reason

I went back home on the holidays. When I'd grow tired of their teasing and disapproving looks that's where I'd wander off to, but they'd grown accustomed to know where I was. So as the years went on they no longer searched, they'd just wait until I came back and claim that I must be over my dramatic tantrum, at least I'd have something real to show Ethan, so when he saw how pretentious my family life actually was, he'd see something beautiful in the midst of all the chaos.

I wasn't thrilled I'd have to venture there alone, it just threw another spanner in the works of what I'd have to worry about tomorrow. I should have learnt to drive years ago and I had given it a go, but when I'd got to the traffic lights and the instructor had got all flustered because I still hadn't moved, I vowed that it just wasn't worth the stress and that public transport was good enough for me because I'd probably end up wrapped around a tree or in some other disaster, but now as I sat on my bed having a car didn't seem so terrifying, it would have certainly come in handy, now that my ride had let me down. Public transport across Christmas, I couldn't think of anything worse.

I just prayed nothing else would go wrong, it was bad enough spending Christmas with the deranged and insane, to top it off I'd be spending most of the day on a train with a bunch of other people who more than likely didn't want to travel, yes this was fine—oh who was I kidding?

This was going to be a disaster.

Nine

Highway To Hell

The journey to hell was long and gruesome. It hadn't started off great, for a start I'd over slept, the damn alarm had never gone off, or maybe I'd never set it, who knows, but all I knew was that I was now late and running around the apartment like a headless chicken. I was feeling the stress already and I hadn't even left the building, when all I wanted to do was crawl back into bed and hide under the covers, my hair was matted to my head and as I look at my horrific appearance in the mirror, I seem to resemble a homeless person, I shake my head as I turn the shower on, my body is trembling because I've forgotten to turn the heating on and in December without the heating on, you may as well be stood outside, cold smoke blows from my mouth with every breath, I really want to just lay in a hot, steamy bath and allow the warmth to envelope me, but due to my very late start the only thing I can do is take a quick shower.

The mad dash to the bus station is as horrifying as I had imagined. I had planned on taking a taxi but with my accidental lateness nobody would come pick me up in time, the bus journey was horrific, have you ever tried standing on public transport that's heaving with a long journey ahead of you, all eyes are on you, you have to hold tight of your luggage lest it roll away and whack someone in the face, while that would make for a hilarious story to tell, it wasn't really something I wanted to live in the grand scheme of things. Your legs ached from standing for so long and you held onto the iron bars like it was your last fucking lifeline, while the passengers bumped and crashed into you as they got on and off the journey to hell, this was a nightmare and I hadn't even arrived yet. I wasn't even halfway there, no I'd not yet got on the next death contraption, I could feel a migraine coming on, the only thing that kept my salvation was eagerly looking as the passengers left the death contraption, hoping to jump and hop into their seat before the next passenger claimed it, it was like fucking whack-a-mole.

Finally, I could breathe, after what felt like a lifetime I finally got to sit down, the sweet release of sitting down almost had me moaning with pleasure, although with the amount of bodies surrounding me I thought it may be oddly placed, a woman getting aroused from sitting down, it was as exciting as taking off your shoes at the end of a shift, or releasing the girls from a contraption we liked to call a 'bra' those things were not made for comfort, a man definitely made those, after all why would a woman make something so torturous for the entire female population.

Looking out of the window thinking of what this weekend had in store for me because I didn't know, I never knew, it was always the greatest surprise, like I said it started out like Disney, then it would turn into a Stanley Kubrick movie, but this was one scene you couldn't escape from. I longed for the comfort of my small apartment, shit, I'd even have preferred to work over Christmas, I was that involved in my own erratic thoughts that I never even knew that someone had plonked themselves on the seat beside me.

"So, what brings you here?" Looking to the side of me there he sat, heavily smelling of pungent alcohol and leering at me with every passing glance as his eyes roam across my body, great, that's all I need, to be seated next to a pervert for the rest of my journey. "Not much of a talker, huh." He slurs. Maybe if I ignore him, he'll go away, but of course—I'm not that lucky. "Hey, I'm talking to you." He shouts more aggressively.

"I chose not to answer." I smirk.

"Oh, she does speak and with the voice of an angel." He sings. I can't help the laugh that falls from my lips, but the young drunken passenger instantly smiles. "That's more like it, after all it is Christmas." Don't remind me, I think as I just smile and nod, after awhile it's plain to see that the drunken passenger is harmless and he was just like me, in need of a seat for the rest of his journey, he happily chats about his family for the next 20 minutes and not to be rude I nod and smile while I listen to the tale of his story, which wasn't at all interesting, but it was just kind to act interested, after all isn't that what Laney Powell did, acted interested in things she wasn't just to please everyone around her, it was my most awful trait, but I just never had the heart to upset others. I'd punish myself forever if I'd thought I'd hurt someone, he kisses my hand before he leaves and once again I'm alone.

Thankfully the rest of my journey is uneventful, the train ride is oddly peaceful with no interruptions and shockingly I even manage to scoop a seat. I was nearing the end of my journey and the flutter started in the pit of my stomach, I wasn't excited, this was a sick, worried feeling, the feeling I always got when I was on my way home for Christmas. I felt a sense of peace as I got off of the train and entered a taxi to the manor, my journey was almost over and in all honestly not as terrible as I had previously thought, the car rolls up to the six foot iron gates, he's instantly buzzed in, I look out of the window at the scenic view as the car rolls down the skinny path towards the house, in the distance through the trees I spot her, the beautiful glittering silver lake and even though I'm home for Christmas I do something I never thought I'd do—I smile.

My mother is standing on the curved marbled steps, looking like Lady of the valley, I roll my eyes as I fetch my luggage from the boot.

"Laney, put those down, Tom will do that, that's what the help is for."

"I don't mind—."

"What would our guests think."

"Perish the thought, mother." She giggles like I've said something funny.

Wrapping her arm around me, she gives me what she'd think would pass as a hug, "you have been keeping secrets from me."

"I have?"

"Why didn't you tell me you had a man? And a man that looks like that." She fake fans her face, "he's positively delicious, and a doctor, wait until I tell everyone, they will be pleased." I squeeze an awkward smile out.

"Oh, he's here?"

"I sent him to your room." She whispers.

Of course, why didn't I think of that, shit, I'd have to share a room with Ethan, but I'm sure he wouldn't mind, it would only be for the weekend.

"Go on, don't keep him waiting."

"Of course not." She squeezes my arm, "oh, you've made me so proud."

Oh of course, getting a nursing degree, going through university, paying off the student loans alone, getting an apartment and making it on my own didn't make her proud, no, but a man did, a fake boyfriend at that, but what she didn't know couldn't hurt her, I was just relieved Ethan had pulled through, the thought of turning up here alone was worse than the train wreck journey to get here.

Walking through the grand double doors, I could already see the room filling up with their guests, guests I'd have to smile and exchange pleasantries with later on, my face would be aching by the end of the night with all the fake smiling I'd have to do.

I could hear my converse tap against the marble floor with every step, it shone to perfection, looking down it was cleaner than a mirror, you could see your reflection in it, Ethan must have really made an impression because she hadn't even shown disgust at my frazzled appearance, usually she'd have ushered me through the back door where the workers were kept, so the guests wouldn't see such an unkempt part of the family, but she'd barely batted an eyelid, maybe this weekend wouldn't be too terrible after all.

Oh I was wrong I think, so very wrong, the thing that was about to burst my perfectly pink bubble was heading straight towards me, long straight blonde hair falls down her shoulders, bright blue eyes widen and a perfectly fake smile sits across her perfectly fake face, huge tits bounce up and down in a figure hugging baby pink body-con dress that can barely contain her slim physique, oh yay, it's barbie, I think as she rushes towards me, blowing air kisses because this is how the pretentious greet each other, "oh darling, how have you been."

"I've—."

"Oh, you have to tell me about that gorgeous man of yours, I took a peek earlier and oh-my-god, how did you land a specimen like that."

Yes, like I was the ogre of the manor, Selena was your typical rich bitch of society, she thought she was the most gorgeous thing that had ever lived, well I can see why, men literally fell at her feet, but she'd never taken a husband, she said she was searching for the right one, but she'd still managed to get through as much dick as she could in her search for 'the perfect man' and it seemed that poor Ethan had caught her eye, unfortunately for her, this man was already taken—and not by me.

"Lucky, I guess."

"Oh you sure are, we—."

"Selena, will you leave the poor girl alone, she's barely got through the door and you're already hounding her."

"Whatever." She flicks her hair across her shoulders and waltzes into the room, probably to go see if she can find another helpless victim.

"Mary." I scream as I run into the middle-aged house keepers arms, her kind brown eyes soften at the sight of me and her rosy plump cheeks push out as her thin lips form into a kind, gentle smile, her arms instantly surround me with warmth as she wraps me in her embrace and finally I feel some semblance of love in the midst of all this chaos.

"Well let me get a look at you." She gushes as she wipes the small tear that has fallen down her cheek, "you look perfect, just as I remember you."

"And you—haven't changed one bit." I smile.

Mary was always like the mother I never got, she was kind, warm and welcoming, she'd make home cooked meals, she was there to listen to your day and when this house was too much and I'd run to the lake, she'd always come and find me, she didn't think I was having a tantrum, she showed me nothing but kindness, she'd practically raised me and I was elated she was still here.

"Go on, you better go get refreshed before the madness starts." I just nodded, Mary knew how I felt about these functions, but she also knew that I'd never miss one out of obligation.

Walking up the winding staircase, I look down at all the smiling faces, dressed in their best, already sizing each other up, getting ready to see who's dick was bigger, honestly I didn't know why I still attended these functions, they traumatized me for weeks after I'd leave, but that wasn't going to happen this time because I had sweet Ethan, I keep telling myself repeatedly as if on repeat, I hoped nobody else would enthrall me in a mindless conversation and that I could just make it to my room with no interruptions because after the day I'd had all I wanted was a little bit of peace before the madness consumed me.

Placing my hand on the golden door knob I was almost home free, turning I'm about to enter, "Laney, how is my little fry." I inwardly groan, I hated that nickname, he knew I hated that nickname but it didn't stop him from saying it every time he saw me.

"Justin." I smile.

"When are you going to marry me."

"Never." I stick my tongue out as a hearty chuckle leaves his throat.

"Well, you know where I am if you change your mind." He winks.

Shaking my head, finally I turn the door knob and enter, closing the door with my back, collapsing against it, I finally breathe, this has been one turmoil after another, Justin was here, that only spelt trouble, when we we're kids he'd tease me something rotten, he had his own company in California but he still managed to travel for these ridiculous events, he said it was good for business, but I didn't see how, after all what business would he have in the countryside. I'm sure it was just a rouse, as he'd gotten older he had flirted and tried crossing the line of our friendship, but I'd made a point of not letting him cross that line, much to his dismay, I'm not sure what he saw in me, I'm sure he'd be much more suited to someone like Selena, it's not that she hadn't tried, but he was probably one of the only people in this house that she hadn't sucked off, maybe it was because he knew I detested her, or maybe he just saw through her Mary fucking sunshine act too. Whatever it was, he hadn't given up on asking me to marry him, he'd bought a ring once, his proposal is probably the closest I'd ever get to a commitment from a man, he was voted the most eligible bachelor in GQ magazine, but I just didn't have those feelings for Justin, I was searching for a spark and as perfect as he was—it just wasn't there.

My suitcase is already laid at the side of the bed, how did I manage to miss Tom from the door to the chaos of getting to my room, well, he always were precise, Tom was Mary's husband, he was a sweetheart of a man, a man of very few words, but he never complained and while he never really brought much to the conversation he was a listener, which was just as well because I'm sure Mary talked the man's ears off, but they'd been married for fifty years, so clearly something in their dynamic had worked. I could only hope to find someone who would want to put up with me for that long I think as I chuckle, although not sure I'd want to share cookie dough, but you never know, the right guy, maybe one day. I start unpacking my suitcase and placing my things in the draws and the wardrobe, I must be in my own little world because I think I'm alone in here, until I feel a hand slide gently up my back.

His hot breath wisps on the nape of my bare neck, sending shivers and leaving goosebumps with each wisp of heat that he leaves, his breathing is erratic and his body is so close to mine, almost touching, but not quite.

"Well, hello princess, I've been waiting for you." His deep sultry whisper pierced my ear, sending flutters to the crevice in between my thighs, spinning around, I see his muscular shoulders, my eyes scan every part of his delicious body, trying to avert my gaze from the obvious bulge between his legs, my breath matches his as my eyes slowly crawl back up his body and settles on those piercing crystalline blue eyes.

"Beau." I utter.

Shit.

Ten

Surprise

What was he doing here?

He wasn't Ethan.

No, I couldn't spend an entire weekend with Beau, not here, in this room, shit, there was only one bed, but as that thought crossed my mind I could feel the dripping between my thighs, no, that was not happening and all I could think was, *where the fuck was Ethan.*

I'm just stood there staring at him, he must see the shock on my face, but instead of comforting me, he's finding some sick enjoyment in my obvious torment because he just stands there with that stupid grin placed upon his face.

"Where is Ethan?" Are the only words I manage to speak.

"With his wife would my guess, I mean honestly, imagine asking a married man to do this." He tuts as if it was the crime of the century, my hands instantly go into my head, while I pace up and down at my newfound turmoil.

"No, no, no." I repeat over and over again.

"You're cute when your stressed." He taps my nose.

"You have to leave—right now."

"Sorry princess, No can do."

"Beau, I'm not playing—leave."

"What would your family think."

"I don't give a fuck what they'd think—I—I can't believe you two would do this to me." I slump down on the bed.

"You're such a funny little elf." Scowling I finally raise my head, "I'm so glad that ridiculous nickname has stuck." I feel him sit beside me, his hand slides up my thigh, I try make out that his touch doesn't effect me but as his hand gently squeezes my thigh, my legs tremble with desire.

"That's not going to work." I whisper.

"No?"

"No." I move his hand away from mine, but he catches my hand in his, "go home Beau, go play your games—."

"I want you."

"Tough shit."

"Laney—."

"Fuck you, Beau." His eyes seem to change, a change in his face can be seen at my harsh words, I'm not sure what, but a change instantly crosses his face, it's just for a split second, but in that second he—looks—well—dangerous, dark and—right now—my body wants him.

"Please—leave." I know I'm weakening, shit, even he knows I'm weakening, I can see it in his face.

"Now why would I want to do that princess." His hand slides gently up my throat and it takes all the willpower I have within me to not moan out loud, but deep within I'm fucking howling, his touch feels heavenly, fuck, I just want his hands to climb down my body and surrender to the bliss I currently find myself in, my heart is racing, palms are sweaty, but that's nothing compared to the way my body trembles for him.

His hand grips my throat, squeezing ever so slightly, his touch is forceful, masterful, alluring with the hidden depths of just the right amount of sensuality as he pulls my head closer to his, "good girl, see now that wasn't so—hard—was it." Oh—fuck. Now all I can think of is his hard cock, there's a pulsing in my head, a dizzying, nauseating feeling overcomes my entire body, he's placing my body across the bed and god dammit! I'm letting him. I can feel his hard body pressed against mine and all thoughts of him leaving have completely left my head, no the only thoughts I have are disgusting, disturbing thoughts, I want this man to fucking ruin me, I can almost taste the sin on his lips, but damn him, he still hasn't pressed them against mine.

I know I need to stop this, after all it's Beau, I can't do this with Beau, of all people, but as he clambers on top of me, parting my legs with his, I'm losing all common sense, my head swims and all I can think about is his hard cock that I can feel digging into my thigh, my breathing is ragged, I know he can see the excitement on my face, his hands grip my wrists and pins them above my head, fuck, I'm soaking as he lowers the rest of his body hard against mine, pressing me further into the mattress, it may as well have just swallowed me up, his legs continue to part mine forcefully, shit, I don't think I've ever been this excited, a long slow growl enters my ear drum and I very nearly cum from the vibrations of his voice, "I can fucking smell your excitement." He breathes.

"Shit, Laney—I'm so fucking hard for you." A loud moan finally escapes my lips. I feel a gush of liquid between my thighs, he nestles his nose into my neck, I feel his hot breath massaging me, "oh fuck, I've never wanted to fuck anyone as badly as I want to fuck you." Another loud moan leaves my body, if he's not careful I'm going to cum just from his words alone.

His mouth finally comes down on mine and I finally get a taste of sin on my lips—and oh—how delicious sin tastes, his tongue enters my mouth and my whole body explodes. I feel his hand release my wrist as it slowly crawls down my body, teasing my hips with his fingertips, slow moans fall into the depths of his mouth, his fingers snake between the crevice of my thighs, he finally dips them gently inside me and—oh sweet heaven, my back arches as I cry out in ecstasy, "fuck, your dripping baby, is this all for me." His fingers reach deeper into my tingling pussy that's begging to be played with, every movement causes a tingle to rise in the pit of my belly back down to the dripping mess, "oh fuck, oh fuck," I cry out between labored breaths. I think the torture is over, but then he curls his fingers deep within my tingling dripping hole and I see fucking stars, the loud bursts of moans fall from my lips, "oh god, Beau, yes, yes, yes." I scream, but he's not done, I feel him snake down my body, his nose nudges up my soaking pussy, I feel his hot tongue snake across my lips, my hips buck at the sudden heat from his tongue, I can barely contain the breathless gasps that fall out, thrashing my hands in his head, his tongue enters me, moving backwards and forwards, pushing his face deeper into my pussy, his tongue settles deep within me, my hips thrust, as his tongue massages me harder and faster, bucking my hips faster, fucking his face within an inch of my life, the tingles turn to explosions. I'm no longer moaning, I'm screaming his name as his tongue lashes faster and faster, the build up is coming, it's like a firework ready to spark and spray the most beautiful color's into the night sky, one more buck of my hips and a few more flicks of his tongue, my back arches off of the bed, as I finally feel the splurge of my pleasure spill out, with nothing but the sound of my screaming to surround us, slick sweat pierces every part of my body. I finally release his head, laying back, bathing in the erotic bliss of being tongue fucked by Beau fucking Rivers.

His head comes up, I half expect him to leave, after all he's finally fucked me, okay, not with his cock, with his delectable tongue and every dirty fantasy I'd had of him in my head over the years was nothing compared to the reality, Beau Rivers, was a fucking machine, it had been years since I'd been touched by a man and when he'd touched me, I'd exploded, the explosion had spread across my body in waves, he was just looking up at me with that stupid grin placed upon his face, "we are not done yet little elf." My eyes widen, shit, was he serious? I'm not sure I had any fluids left inside of me after that display of pure fucking pleasure, but the way he was looking at me had me dripping once more, how was it possible that he didn't even need to touch me to cause the dam to break, just one look and I was ready for him.

"Beau—."

"Oh, no you don't little elf." He smiles.

"Stop overthinking, you're not allowed to think, the only thing you need to do my little flesh light is to feel how full you feel with my cock buried deep inside of you."

Shit, I didn't even have a response, I just stared at him with wide eyes, nobody had ever spoken to me like that, it was crude, it was disgusting, but the tingles between my legs tell me that every crude, disgusting word makes my body tremble with desire.

I shouldn't be doing this, I know, a little bit late for that, I just got caught up in the moment, tangled beneath Beau's tongue, drowning in Beau's taste, no this was a mistake, I should just—but Beau is now standing before me, muscular, pristine, his skin seems to glisten under the lighting in the room, my eyes roam across every delectable curve and muscle of this glorious specimen in front of me, there isn't an ounce of fat on his ridiculously ripped body, my tongue snakes across my lips, he looks positively delicious, no snap out of it I try tell myself, but as my eyes roam lower I can't help the desire that crawls up my body, his very thick, hard cock is pulsing, I want to look away, I should look away, but I'm hypnotized by Beau's delicious cock.

His hand slivers across my body, parting each clothing away from my skin, I'm raw, open, exposed. His eyes roam across every inch of my body as I lay there open, exposed, he's got me right where he wants me, I want to get up, I want to leave, but the way he's looking at me renders me unable to move, he gently bites his lip as he looks down at me and that's all it takes for a soft moan to pass my lips, he takes this as an invitation, within moments he's crawled on top of me, parting my legs wider than they have ever been parted, I can feel the twinge of the muscle on my thigh as he stretches me wide, I can feel him pressing the head of his cock at my centre, an instant searing pain jolts me as he pushes his thick head into my centre, a small gasp leaves my lips, "almost there, baby." My arms lazily fall down his back as he slowly penetrates his thick cock deep within me, "fuck baby, you're so fucking tight." He breathes, the moment his cock enters me, I instantly feel full, his cock hits my cervix as a scream erupts from the back of my throat, slowly thrusting his hips, he moves deeper within me, the pleasure crashes over me in waves, my back arches, another scream rips from my throat, his large hands come across my mouth, my pussy clenches at the lack of air I now feel, but as he thrusts while restricting my airways, the excitement crawls higher and higher, "oh fuck, your pussy feels so amazing, that's it Laney, fucking scream, nobody can hear you." He whispers. My body shakes in responses to his words, pushing deeper I feel my pussy contract harder around his cock, he's gasping now, moving faster and deeper within me, his body is sticky and slick with sweat as it mashes against mine. I can feel my hot breath against my skin as I scream into his hand, the pleasure runs through my body harder and faster, "oh fuck, you feel so fucking good," he coos in my ear, "god, you're so—fucking—tight." He gasps, harder and harder I scream with every thrust of his hips, his cock filling me up, our bodies rock backwards and forwards in a frenzy of lust and passion, the heat crawls through my cervix straight to my heart, one more push and a long, slow scream gets drowned out into his hand, a rush of juices crawls across his cock, coating him in my desire and straight down my thighs, "oh fuck, I'm—I'm—cumming—." I hear him scream as his hot cum sprays across the inside of my vagina walls, his breathing is ragged as he gasps for breath, finally releasing his hand from my mouth, a rush of oxygen enters my airways and the blood rushes straight to my head as he collapses on top of me.

"That—was—fucking—amazing." He gasps.

"Finally got what you wanted?"

"No."

"So, you didn't want to fuck me?"

"What, yes of course I did."

"So, you got what you wanted."

"I only ever wanted you."

"I'm sure that's what you say to all of them."

"Fuck, everything was perfect."

"Was?"

"Yeah, until you opened your fucking mouth."

Not so perfect after all, I think, but having him lay across my chest, even with my smart remarks, warmth spreads across my heart and I knew it, I knew that this would happen if I ever let him in my bed, I knew I'd fall for him because hadn't that already happened all those years ago, I'd fallen for him, that's where my vendetta against Beau had come from, it was never hate, it was disappointment. I was disappointed that he'd never gave it a chance, instead he'd run away and I'd never know if we could have made it work, it was easier to admit to myself that I hated Beau.

But I didn't.

Not even a little bit.

Not at all.

Eleven

I Love To Hate You

Waking up, I wonder if last night's events were just a dream, sure felt like something you'd dream up in your head.

"Good morning." He smiles at the side of me, Beau is in my bed, Beau is naked in my bed, pulling the covers up to gaze down at my body, shit, I'm naked in bed with Beau, I shake my head.

"Can you turn around."

"Why?"

"I'm naked." I whisper.

"I know, I remember removing your clothes before I fucked you." He whispers back.

Shit, shit, shit, shit.

Wrapping the sheet around my body, sliding my legs off of the bed, I'm home free I think with a smile, standing I feel a tug on the white sheet as my face suddenly turns to horror the sheet slides down back onto the bed, leaving me exposed, Beau looks at me with that wicked grin, while sliding his tongue across his lips, laying back onto the plush pillow with his hands behind his head, his eyes continue to roam across my body, "now, that's what I call a morning surprise."

"Beau, you asshole." I scream forgetting for a moment that I'm completely naked, stamping my feet, I know, I know what I probably look like but he's purposefully embarrassed me, for what? His sick entertainment, stamping into the bathroom I slam the door behind me, I half expect him to follow me in here, but he doesn't.

Holding on to the sink as I try take deep breaths, I can't understand why he repeatedly taunts me, he'd got what he wanted, he'd fucked me, so what was he still doing here? I'd half expected to wake up alone, but clearly he hadn't tortured me enough, well one thing was for sure, there would not be a repeat of what happened last night.

Turning on the shower, as I step in, instantly feeling the warmth as the water gently cascades down my body, the water soothes the annoyance that Beau has caused, I feel arms come around me, instantly I jump, the water drips into my eyes as I crash into the wall, "what the hell Beau, get out, now."

"You're funny."

"I'm not joking," I scream while pushing against his chest, "get out."

"Are you sure that's what you want."

"Yes, now, Le—." A small moan crawls from my body as his fingers flick and tease my hardened nipples, dipping his head under the water his tongue flicks across causing shivers to erupt inside of me once again, "are you sure?" He smiles.

"We are not doing this again—."

"Doing what?" His fingertips crawl down my body, moving his hands they rest firmly beneath my buttocks, lifting me in the air, he catches my mouth with his, mumbling through his kiss, his mouth finally releases mine, "yes?"

"Last night—." He moves my legs to wrap around his waist, as he pushes my body further into the tiled wall, "we are not repeating last night—." I breathlessly gasp.

"Of course not," I can feel him pressing his engorged head right near my wet hole, his arms move round my back, pushing down on my shoulders, feeling myself lower onto his hard cock, I cry out as he finally enters me, "last night I fucked you in the bedroom," he whispers, while pushing his cock further inside of me, "today I'm fucking you in the bathroom," his cock moves slowly, hitting the spot instantly, the pleasures crawls up my body and out of my mouth, "that's not a repeat, but I am still going to fuck you," he breathes into my ear, "how could I not, Laney, you're so fucking delicious," my labored breaths come thick and fast, feeling his body so close to mine causes my body to melt against his, the harder he moves inside of me, the louder my groans of pleasure fill the air, "oh fuck baby, my favorite place is inside of you," he cries out, my head falls onto his shoulder, biting down hard, he rams into my swollen pussy harder, each movement he makes within me causes a burst of pleasure just waiting to erupt, "oh Beau, oh—my—god," my muffled cries call into his shoulder, one more thrust and he pours all of his excitement deep inside me, our bodies shake as the last slip of pleasure ejects from our slippery bodies.

Breathless he holds onto my body waiting for the tremors to slow in my body, gently he unwraps my legs from around my body and places me back gently on the tiled floored surface, still catching my breath, I lean into the wall, he'd done it again, within moments he'd took my breath away, every moment with Beau was bittersweet, it had to come to an end at some point and he was just delaying the inevitable. Turning I face the water to finish what I had started before he came in here waving around his magic wand, standing back under the water, allowing the water to once again cascade down my body, I feel something soft move in circles around my back, "what are you doing now," he leans into my back, "I made you dirty baby, now I'm getting you all—clean." God, he knew no bounds, Beau definitely didn't abide by personal space, but as he runs the soapy sponge down my back I very nearly melt, his touch feels like magic, it's heavenly. Well I suppose it couldn't hurt to allow him to wash my back, then he was definitely leaving, he runs the soapy sponge in small circular movements around my entire body, parting my legs with his hand, he runs the sponge up my inner thighs, something as innocent as this has my body shaking once more with anticipation, he gently runs the sponge across my pussy, parting my legs wider he moves it up and down across my lips, pushing his finger hard across the sponge, "oh fuck, what are you doing." He leaves a trail of kisses across my bare shoulder, "I told you, you're dirty baby, you need to be clean." He continues this assault on my bare, sensitive, now dripping pussy, the moans spill out of my mouth, he's slowing down but the pleasure has taken over, holding his hand I remove the sponge, letting it fall to the ground, allowing his fingers to dip inside of me, once again allowing Beau to tip me over the edge.

"This can't happen again."

"But you seem to like it—so much." He's moved away from the door, holding the towel up, driving it across his wet hair, "Beau, I mean it, that was the last time," he laughs, "isn't that what you said the first time." Turning off the water, I grab for my own towel, gently wrapping the cotton around my body, "Beau, I mean it, that was the last time."

"Why do you pretend like you hate me."

"I do hate you,"

"You love to pretend to hate me, but we both know you love me really," he winks.

"Get out." I scream while flinging a towel in Beau's direction, he merely slides out of the way, with a wicked smile on his face as he walks through the door closing it at the perfect moment, allowing the towel to skim across the door, falling to the ground.

He infuriated me, I'd love to wipe that smug smile off of his perfectly chiseled face, imagine having the balls to say what he just said to me, he was going to drive me crazy this weekend, it appeared I'd been letting him, but not no more, no, this couldn't happen again, once was bad enough, but twice—what is it that they said? Once was a mistake, but twice was a choice.

Is that what I was doing?

Was I choosing to allow Beau free reign over my body?

Then if it was a choice, then I could easily choose not to allow it to happen again, choice? Such a simple word, but when he touched me my body came alive, with every light touch its like his fingers told a secret only my body knew how to decipher, with every dance his fingers sang a song straight to my soul, like a hidden song, a mystery you'd try decipher, but knew you never would, maybe I just wouldn't let him touch me, but everything about him drew me in, his voice, his scent, his touch, oh-my-god, his touch.

But I'd had him, twice now, the itch that I'd been wanting to scratch for years was well and truly scratched, but as I remember the fleeting moments we've had, the tingling between my thighs reminds me that any moment with Beau would never be enough, but I can't go down this road with him, I can't get too comfortable with him, not like this, I had to end it before I couldn't, before I started dreaming of what life with Beau would be like, I had to put a stop to whatever the fuck this was, I'd just have to be strong and say goodbye to the magic wand between his legs, "do you hear that," I look down between my legs,"no more magic stick," god, I was actually crazy, not in a 'I'm so cute and kooky crazy,' the kind of crazy where you sit in a padded cell. I mean you had to be crazy if you were having conversations with your vagina, like it would even listen I think while rolling my eyes.

No, I had decided my vagina didn't get a say, after all she wouldn't care when it all fell apart, this was not up to the vagina, this was a choice I had to make, if nothing else, for my own sanity.

It was so much simpler when I'd hated Beau, before he'd touched me and opened up a world of feelings, yes, to go back to the days of hating Beau would have been so much more simpler, but the only person I was fooling there was myself, I mean Beau himself even knew I didn't hate him, had he known the entire time, what was he doing all those years, humoring me?

I suppose it had been a fun little game, a game that had gone on for far too long, a game that even our friends were sick of seeing, there was only so long you could play a game of hate, at some point you'd have to be honest, if not with anyone else, at the very least yourself.

I suppose I could be more civil to Beau, after all he'd been inside of me on multiple times, I'm sure there was a friendship in there somewhere, but how do you be friends with someone who makes you tremble without even touching you, practice I'd guess, after all I'd practiced hating him and that had worked for five years—or had it? I just didn't know anymore, the longer I spent with Beau, the more crazy I felt. I was doing things I wouldn't normally do, saying things I wouldn't normally say, I wasn't sure if that was a good thing or a bad thing, but one things for sure, Beau made me crazy.

I mean here I was, in the bathroom after Beau had fucked me once again, arguing with myself about the situation I should never have allowed myself to be put in, no, I'd decided, I didn't care what he said, I'd resist his charms—somehow, he'd had me, twice and there would not be a third time. I would go back to hating Beau, it was much simpler, I smile at my genius plan, this would work I tell myself, unsure if I was as confident as my head was telling me I was, but confident or not...

I wasn't going to sleep with Beau Rivers ever again.

Twelve

Dinner With The Kranks

How was I supposed act now?

I had done what I swore I'd never do—I had fucked Beau, how could I go back to work and look him in the eyes without seeing his body mashed against mine, without feeling the sheer pleasure his cock had given me when he had penetrated me, how could I listen to his voice without hearing that deep sexy growl in my ear, there were so many things I couldn't do and all because I'd fucked Beau.

As I sat next to him at the dining table with my family awaiting the lavish meal that I'd have to get through and listen to the mind numbing idiotic conversation that would more than likely kill a few brain cells, suddenly I felt out of place, well, here, I always felt out of place, but next to Beau, I just didn't know how to act. I was at a loss of what was customary behavior after you'd fucked your archenemy, how was you supposed to act, he was looking at me rather strangely, probably thought I was nuts, I was, why had I fucked Beau, it couldn't end well, history told me that.

"Hey, are you okay?" He whispers.

"Fine." I muster a side smile, but I know I'm not fooling him.

"How did you two meet?" My mother questions across the table, then suddenly all eyes are on us, Inwardly I groan, but why was I surprised, this was the first man I'd ever brought home and it wasn't even the right one, it was the wrong boyfriend for Christmas that had turned up, he was a complete surprise, but nothing surprised me more than the fact that I'd already let him fuck me on the first day I'd gotten here, maybe it was always going to happen, the build up had been coming for a long time and while I'd pictured it repeatedly in my head, I'd never thought it would actually happen, be careful what you wish for—I guess.

"We work together."

"Oh, we met long before then." Beau smiles.

"Nobody wants to hear that." I grit.

"We do, we do." They all cry out in unison.

"See, they do." He pats my nose with the tip of his finger, instantly I wrinkle my nose under his touch, his mouth comes down on mine, gasping into his mouth, he starts telling a long tale of how we met, for the most part his story is true, I don't hear half of what he says because I'm trying to calm my breath from the intoxicating kiss he's just placed upon my lips, I only know it must be good because they're all gushing and hanging on his every word, he's enchanted everyone in the room, well, everyone except Justin.

"It's strange, Laney has never mentioned you." Justin calls out.

"That is strange, but come to think of it, Laney has never mentioned you either, what's your name again?" Beau at his finest, now I was just waiting for them to whip out their dicks at the dinner table to decide who's dick was the biggest. I was just waiting for the dueling to start, swords at the ready gentlemen, god I was ridiculous, imagine, these two men fighting for my affections, it was almost laughable, considering I'd never end up with either of them.

They went back to their moronic conversations and I sat there in silence poking at my bloody lamb as I did every year, I mean honestly, who wanted to eat a bleeding carcass, think I'd rather throw up in my own mouth than stick that anywhere near my mouth, but as I look around the table they are all devouring it like it's the tastiest morsel on earth, to me they just looked like a bunch of cannibals enjoying their sacrificed victim. I shake my head, I'd hoped that by bringing someone with me it would help fill the silence that now ensued, but the man I'd planned on bringing wasn't here and I'd already fucked the surprise guest, this day had just gotten worse and worse as it went on, pushing back my chair I hear the scrape as it moves across the hardwood flooring, standing, all eyes are on me, I gulp, "I have a headache, may I be excused." I divert my eyes towards my mother because she's basically running the show, she just simply nods, as I turn Beau places his hand on mine, looking into his eyes, all I can see is worry across his face, "I'm fine, I'm just going to lie down, it's been a long day." I lie, he nods, making a move to get up, "No, you should stay, at least for dessert."

He smiles, "are you sure?" I'm not sure if his gentleman prose is an act or genuine, I merely just smile, "I insist." I smile back at him as I turn and walk away before anyone else can stop me from leaving.

Closing the door behind me, I can finally breathe, collapsing against the dark oak door, I finally take a breath, closing my eyes, hoping I will be transported back home and this nightmare will be finally over, opening my eyes gently a big smile greets me, "didn't like the food?" Mary asks, I don't want to offend the poor woman but I can't help the grimace I pull when she mentions the living dead sat on plates in the other room, "I just prefer my meat—."

"Cooked." We both say in unison.

"I can—." I shake my head, "No, I'm fine, I'm actually really tired, I just want to lay down and go to sleep."

"You know where I am if you change your mind." Wrapping my arms around her, I pull her in, holding onto her, I finally find comfort in the arms of a woman that treated me more like a daughter than my own mother ever did, my mother always said hugs were for people who didn't have a grasp on life, she was the only person I knew who could take a simple act of love and kindness and turn it into something hideous.

The walk to my room was a peaceful one, I wondered how Beau was getting on in the room of doom, but he'd stayed so it can't have been that tragic, I'm sure Selena would have pounced at the chance to maul him the moment I'd left, he'd probably have his hands all over her, basking in the attention she'd be giving him, they were more suited than he and I was, shit, what was I saying? When did I turn into this jealous, needy pathetic woman? Why did I care what Beau did all of a sudden, had I not watched him flirt with girls repeatedly over the years, sure I'd been disgusted but I'd never given it a second thought, no, I didn't care what Beau did, but that was a lie, I did care what he did. I cared even more now because of what we had done, he'd crawled under my skin within mere moments of me entering this room, he'd touched me in places I'd never been touched before, I knew he was going to ruin me the moment he touched my skin, but I'd let him because as much as I'd wanted to deny it to myself, I'd wanted him. I'd wanted him since that first day I'd laid eyes on him five years ago, and now that I'd had him, I wanted more of him, I was going down a road I swore I wouldn't go down because when he rejected me as I knew he would, it was inevitable, he'd break me, something inside would break and I knew if it broke then I'd never be able to crawl back out into the light, he'd touched the dark places of my soul, every whisper, every growl, every teasing touch had crawled its way into my heart, within moments he'd completely enchanted me and ruined me for anyone else, I sigh as I let my dress fall to the ground, peeling the underwear from my skin I climb into bed, allowing the soft covers to wrap me into a peaceful embrace.

Before my eyes close I make a promise to myself, what happened with Beau will never happen again, there would be no repeat performance, it was a moment of weakness, a moment I didn't plan on committing a second time.

It's dark when my eyes flutter open, a tingling feeling rouses me from my peaceful slumber, making its way up my thighs, tingles shoot up and down my pussy, crying out from the pleasure that racks my body unable to move, I look down and Beau is between my legs, smiling, "Beau—." I gasp."shhhh princess, I'm going to make it all better."

Was I dreaming? I had to be dreaming, after all hadn't I already promised myself earlier before I'd shut my eyes that this wouldn't happen again, that this couldn't happen again, no, we needed some semblance of normality, what did normal look like with Beau? Where I pretended to hate him and he pretended to not know that he knew I didn't hate him, it was like some tragic soap opera where you knew they'd get together but they danced around the issue for so long, you started to not care whether it happened or not, but it had happened, it had happened earlier and it appeared it was happening again, after all I wasn't stopping him, even though I knew I should, each tantalizing lash of his tongue, each feather light touch from his fingertips were sending me into a frenzy, well why shouldn't I enjoy it, after all when this weekend was over it would be back to normality and if this delicious man wanted to ravage me all weekend—well, I was going to let him.

His fingers dip into my tingling center, "Christ, you're fucking wet already," he breathes into my neck, "god, I love the way you respond to me little elf," a self satisfying moan escapes my lips, "aah." Once again I'm in Beau heaven. His hands crawl up my body, he's not going deep this time, every touch, every movement is slow, this is not rushed, there's no desperate frenzy, he's taking his time and I can feel every light touch, his fingers burn a passion within my skin, holding my hips firmly he's tilting my hips towards his, he slowly moves his thick cock within my dripping hole, this time there's no pain, just pure pleasure, as my body instantly comes alive with the slow, steady erotic movements, my eyes start to flutter close, his hand comes under my chin, "oh no princess, I want you to look at me while I fuck you, embed a memory of this moment into your very fucking soul, each time you close your eyes, you'll remember this moment, you and I, just like this." A small gasp leaves my body, yes, I was right, Beau Rivers was going to fucking ruin me.

His body presses harder into mine, the urge to shut my eyes is strong, but the words he spoke are so much more stronger, staring into his crystalline blue eyes, as the moans gently escape my body, feeling him slowly thrust as his hips meet mine, his thick cock bouncing against my cervix, the pleasure rises, looking into his eyes as he completely claims my body with his, with each thrust I'm falling deeper and deeper over the edge, the way he stares right back sends a tingle into my heart, the warmth spreads with each moment I look into his eyes, the pleasure falls from my lips like he's entered my soul, with every thrust, every gasp, every deep gaze, I'm falling deeper and deeper into the vortex, filled with only Beau on my mind, he wanted to create a memory, he'd created a whole universe, one more thrust and I cry out sobs of pleasure, the tears fall gently down my face as I finally release and cover his cock with my cum, "you did so good princess, now you're mine." He whispers, like that was the plan all along.

Thirteen

Sneaky Selena

I'm roused from my sleep by a knock on the door, it's still dark out, Laney is still sleeping soundly beside me, just glancing at her my heart skips a beat, the rise and fall of her chest as she sleeps peacefully, my eyes roam across her creamy skin, god, she's fucking perfect! Another knock, I groan, who would even be knocking on the door at this hour.

Begrudgingly I find my gray sweats and put them on as I quietly open the door, poking my head out, there is nobody there, was I hearing things, I'm about to close the door and slide back in-between Laney when I'm pulled into the landing, it's dimly lit, but as I look in front of me, there she is stood, shit.

Her hand crawls down my stomach, grabbing hold of her arm, she pouts as she flutters her eyelashes at me, her long blonde hair cascades down her body, barely covering her exposed breasts, my eyes quickly glance and she's stood there completely naked, closing the door behind me, she offers a smile, why the fuck was she smiling?

"My room is over there." She whispers. I smile, oh what a tempting offer, she was offering me to go to her room in the middle of the night, this kind of shit didn't really happen, I shake my head, just when I thought Laney's family couldn't get any worse, I stand corrected.

"That's nice, you better get going then."

"Are you coming?"

"No thanks, I already did that."

"Come on, I've heard you in there, I'd like to sample you—." Her fingernail trails across my chest, "myself."

Was she serious? Was this some sick test, couldn't be, Laney had spoke in length at her distaste for Selena, I mean she had some big balls, what if Laney had answered the door, what would her excuse have been then, but it appeared she'd been listening to everything that had happened between us, how fucking weird.

"Selena, I've tried telling you nicely—."

"You can't tell me you don't want me." She purrs while dragging my hand across her hair, exposing her voluptous chest, her hand once more drags across my chest, instantly I remove it, I've never met a woman as thirsty as this and years ago when I was in Uni I'd have loved this kind of forward woman stood naked in front of me, but not now, I'd already found what I wanted and it wasn't whatever this shit show was.

"Clearly you don't take no for an answer—."

"Men don't usually say no." I almost have to laugh at that comment, sure she was attractive, but there was nothing special about her, nothing that drew you in, I could point out hundreds of carbon copies at the club, men didn't say no because she acted like this, of course they'd jump at the chance to have one guilt free night with a girl who wanted no strings, but I wasn't that man.

"Then this will be a first for you."

"You're really turning me down." I nod, "If you're worried about Laney—she stands on her toes leaning into my ear, "it can be our little secret." She whispers.

Pushing her gently she rocks on the balls of her feet, "Selena, I'm sure one night with you would be like heaven, I'm sure you'd be a fun, dirty little secret, that's all you'd be, there are millions of girls—just like you, worthless, not worth much, just a place to keep your cock warm for the night, I mean what kind of person would act this dick hungry that they'd try sleeping with their cousins boyfriend behind there back, that's the difference between you and Laney, she has class and—well you don't, so thanks for the offer, but I'm not interested.

She just stares at me with her mouth wide open, her eyes fill with water, but I don't feel guilty, if I was the only man in her life to tell her this, hopefully she'd learn a lesson and if she didn't, what did I care, as long as she left me the hell alone I didn't care.

"Your dick probably doesn't work anyway." She spits at me.

"Sure princess, that's why you were just begging for it."

She stamps her feet in front of me, honestly if I didn't know any better I'd have thought a child was stood in front of me, waving her head as a high pitch scream erupts from her throat, stamping to her room, she slams the door.

"Night princess." I smile.

God, this whole weekend had been a nightmare, I'd never seen a family like it before, it was like I'd signed up to join the circus without actually knowing what that entailed, when I'd asked Ethan what his task was he'd only told me that I had to go to Laney's parents for Christmas and pretend to be her boyfriend, it seemed like the perfect opportunity for me to finally win her heart, but this, this I hadn't been warned about, yes, one thing was certain, Laney's family was completely nuts.

Walking back into the room, Laney is still sleeping sounding, I'm glad she didn't witness that, I was horrified by that display I couldn't imagine how it would make Laney feel, it seemed like Laney's family only had one goal, to hurt and disappoint her, it was sad really, a family is supposed to love and care for you, but in my short time here, I'd seen no love, no wonder she didn't come here often, in fact I was unsure why she still came here at all, but she wasn't like her family, she had a big heart, it was one of her best qualities and she had many.

Sliding back in beside her, she doesn't even know I've left, which is just as well, I half contemplate if I should tell her what has just occurred, but I don't want to hurt her, her family does enough of that, it's best this is never mentioned again, after all it's not like I'd be making this a yearly habit, once was enough with the crazy bunch, they made silent hill seem like Disney world, yeah I'd keep one secret from her but only because I never wanted to mention it again, it was ridiculous the lengths they would go to just to hurt her, so tonight I'd protect her from this rather embarrassing act that has ensued.

The girl made my skin crawl, the fact that she thought by standing there naked, I'd just climb into her bed was humorous, what did she think I was, well it appeared she thought exactly what Laney thought I was, but I'd prove her wrong, I'd prove them all wrong, I had eyes for one girl and one girl only and she was laying right beside me.

Moving my arm around her body, pulling her closer so I could smell the intoxicating smells that always evaporated from her skin, she turns to face me with her eyes still closed, mumbling, while nestling her face into my chest and that's when I do it, I relax into her touch, feeling her body so close to mine the heat instantly spreads across my chest, she was so worried about letting me in because she was scared that I'd hurt her, but she didn't see that it was really me that was vulnerable, she'd brought me to my knees, broke down every wall I'd ever had up, I was the one who should be scared because giving her my heart, I was ultimately giving her the power to destroy me. I should have been scared, but I wasn't, I'd give her every piece of me, I'd let her destroy me, if I could only have moments like this, I'd let her destroy me, I didn't care, as long as I could be here like this with her, I'd gave her that power because I'd given my heart away to her a long time ago, she just never realised it.

Fourteen

Silver Lake Dreaming

I'd arose early, with the sun streaming through letting in small cracks of light to let me know morning had arose, Beau was sleeping soundly at the side of me, strange, never thought I'd see that, like ever, maybe he was right, miracles do happen.

The way he touched me embedded a memory into my soul, like a secret I could keep deep within myself to revisit later when he was more than likely gone, I was setting myself up for heartache, I knew that, but try as I might, I just couldn't stop myself when it came to Beau, he was like a sin, he devoured you and uncovered every part of you that you had kept hidden, he was sinful and tempting, a forbidden flower that you knew you shouldn't pick, but against all odds you'd pick it anyway.

Yes, Beau was my sinful desire I think while sat in the kitchen blowing on my black coffee, not a soul in sight, this was when the house was at its most grandest, when the world slept, the creaks and sounds of the old Manor always made me think the house was alive, like it knew things you possibly could not and when it was as quiet as it was right now, it was like the house was whispering all of it's secrets, secrets untold, secrets long forgotten, just a secret between you and the house.

When I was a child, just a young girl with silly thoughts, silly dreams, I'd sometimes sit here and listen to the noises and creaks the house made while everyone was sleeping, I'd listen to the whispers of the old Manor and I'd whisper my own secrets right back, I'd always smile because the house knew my secrets, but I also knew, the house would never tell.

"You're up early." I see Mary smiling as she puts on her flowery apron and starts pottering about the kitchen.

I guess me and the house would have to speak another time, it seemed that the house was no longer asleep.

"You know I don't like to waste time in bed." I smile.

"So what will it be?"

"Oh, you don't need to do that—."

"Its my job." She laughs, "pancakes?" I want to tell her I'm fine, that she doesn't need to make a fuss of me, after all, she's part of the family, even though my mother still referred to her as 'the help' but truth be told she'd be lost without Mary and she knew it, not that she'd ever admit to it, suddenly I hear a loud grumble in the pit of my empty stomach, looking down, I smile, "sure, why not."

The pancakes melt in my mouth, they are just like I remember them, buttery and sweet, the tantalizing taste of buttery pancakes as they slide down my throat makes me groan out loud with every delicious bite, the taste instantly takes me back to my childhood, I used to sit here just like this with Mary when the house was quiet, silently enjoying the delicious treat with the morning sun beaming through the large window panes.

"Feeling better?"

"Much, thank you." I really was grateful, it's strange, I hadn't even felt hungry, but I sure had worked up an appetite, must have been all the sex my body wasn't used to.

"So, tell me about that man of yours."

"He's not really mine." I honestly tell her, after all I can't bare to lie to her, she has one of those faces where you can't help but be honest, she's so kind and welcoming, it would be a cardinal sin to lie to someone like Mary.

"Does he know that." Her eyebrows raise, "know what?" She shakes her head at me, "that he's not really yours." I nod, "well, I've seen a man in love and that man, my dear is absolutely besotted." She walks off to get on with her work, leaving me once again alone with my thoughts.

That couldn't be true, I think I'd have known if Beau had feelings for me wouldn't I?

No, I wasn't stepping to the crazy place, he was just keeping up the charade, Ethan clearly couldn't make it so Beau stepped in, he'd only fucked me because that's what he'd been trying to do for months now, there was no meaning to it, I shake my head, "I wonder where she gets these crazy ideas from, probably her books."

It was just sex, it couldn't be anything more, after all, Beau didn't do relationships, not anymore, isn't that what he had said, yes, that's all this was, just a holiday fling and when we went back we'd forget it ever happened, well he would, I don't think I'd ever be able to forget, I needed some air, I needed to get out of here, get out of my head, and I knew just the place to go to find peace.

"Hey Laney." I look up and see a pristine Selena, god even this early in the morning she looked perfect, did she roll out of bed and flick her hand and in one swift movement perfection ensued, god I hated her, whatever happened to women looking like real women, grabbing an old shirt and sweats, bunching your hair in a messy bun to eat breakfast, after all who would you possibly bump into? Maybe she had it right though, she made an effort, is that what I was supposed to be doing? Nah, why ruin perfection I think with a smile.

"Hey."

"Where is that delicious man of yours?" I had to hand it to her, this was the most she'd ever spoke to me, of course I knew why, because I'd brought eye candy, I'd brought something she wanted, she couldn't have been less obvious if she tried.

"Sleeping."

"Yes, I couldn't help hearing—." Oh of course she couldn't, I'd be shocked if she didn't have a glass pressed against the door. "The good loving—."

"Yes, thank you Selena."

"I'm just saying—he clearly knows how to—please a woman."

Oh my god, could she be anymore transparent, I'm not sure why she was even still invited to these functions, she was just cock hungry and clearly Beau had piqued her interest, shit, why did I even care, it's not like he was mine, was it?

"Anyway, I just wanted to congratulate you on getting good dick, it's not easy to find." She waltzes out of the kitchen after her very crude statement and her words hang in the air.

Getting good dick? Who even thought to say something like that to someone, I mean she wasn't wrong, but why would anyone ever say that? Congratulations, like I'd won the fucking lottery, I shake my head, god no wonder she couldn't keep a man, she was a bloody nightmare.

Placing my coat around my body instantly the warmth comforts me, "going somewhere?" Looking up there is Mary once again, "my favourite spot." I wink.

"You don't want to wait for—." She points towards the ceiling, "No, I would rather go alone." I smile, hoping that she gets the message that I don't want to share my secret spot with anyone—not even Beau.

Walking into the cool winter breeze I can finally breathe, the air had always felt stiff inside the Manor, like your air supply was slowly been cut off, but once you stepped passed the threshold into the great outdoors there was always a sense of calm, peace and serenity, of course it had nothing to do with the Manor, more the people that resided inside of it.

The air around me swirls, picking up the fallen leaves and swirling them in the cool breeze like they were been swallowed in a winter vortex, the clear skies reminded me of Beau's glistening crystalline blue eyes with cracks of sunlight begging to be pushed out, walking into the clearing of the wooded area surround by trees and greenery, the air moved different, almost magical, hearing nothing but the crunch of leaves and twigs beneath my feet with every step I took.

The walk from the house through the wooded area was peaceful and serene, I'd always felt more like the outdoors were home more than the Manor ever was, coming to the end of the woods the trees curved into an alcove shape, little roses would sprout and cover the alcove in the summer months, walking through it felt like you were stepping through to wonderland, stepping through the alcove I see the object of my desire, the one reason that made coming here worth it, there she sat **Silver Lake,** she immediately took my breath away, this was the most beautiful feature of the Manor, it was like the place you'd go to find your soul, sitting down on the grassy area just in front of the lake, I finally take a breath and marvel at the beauty of **Silver Lake.**

I'd always come here to think, that special place you'd go, everyone had one, the one place you could escape, to get a clearer head, as the cold wind blew around my body, looking into the glistening of the lake, the ripples of movement from the water rendered me mesmerized, I couldn't tear my eyes away as I stared into the magical silver lagoon of the lake.

I wasn't sure what was happening with Beau, I felt like I'd fallen into an alternate reality, I mean me and Beau, it was ridiculous, but the connection was there I could feel it, but how far could a connection get you? What would life be like when we left here? There was only one day left and it had seemed so much had happened in that one day, I secretly wish that Ethan had showed up because then I wouldn't be stuck with the dilemma I was currently in, but we hadn't discussed what this even was, if it was anything at all, he'd just ravaged me at every chance he'd gotten, not that I was complaining because Beau had a magic dick, anytime he entered me it was like I was transported to another dimension. Beau and his magic stick, I almost laugh at the very thought, but you know what they said about men with a magic stick, they'd fuck your heart—literally, maybe I was just over thinking the entire thing, maybe I should just enjoy it and go with the glow, enjoy my little weekend fling and then just business as usual, after all why shouldn't I enjoy his magic stick, pretty soon him and his magic stick would once again disappear from my life, yes I would enjoy it—for now.

Laying back onto the dewy grass, I feel the damp grass crawl up my back, it's strange it doesn't make me want to move, it's actually comforting and refreshing, looking into the sky, I sigh, "nothing ever lasts forever." I say to the sky as I close my eyes.

Fifteen

Dreaming Of Laney

When I'd come here I knew she'd be shocked, in fact I was unsure what her reaction would be, after all she was expecting Ethan and what she'd got was—me.

I wasn't planning on fucking her, but every time I was near her I'd just see those big eyes full of innocence and I'd fucking melt, I'd fucked her repeatedly in my head, too many times to count, Laney was like my secret fantasy, I'd expected her to stop me, I wanted her to stop me because I knew once we'd passed that point in our dysfunctional relationship there was no going back and why would I want to, she felt and tasted like fucking heaven.

Waking up, I'd planned to give her a repeat performance of last night, I craved her, I couldn't get enough of her, she even haunted my dreams, I'd awoken to a raging hard on, dreaming of fucking her once more, that's how you knew you had it bad, when you were dreaming about a girl you'd just fucked, but she wasn't any girl—she was Laney.

Instead of getting lost in her, I was disappointed, I was met with an empty bed and silence, she'd got up and left me here, but as I look at the clock on her night stand it's still early, so she can't have left that long ago surely, god, why did she constantly run from me, wasn't that usually the guys job, our dynamic was fucked, now I'd have to go hunt her down and find out what I'd done to piss her off this time.

After a quick shower I race down the stairs, everyone is just getting up it seems, running into the kitchen I see a plump lady cleaning the kitchen counter, sure, I think, she looks friendly enough.

"Oh, if it isn't Laney's Beau." She smiles at her own joke.

"Have you seen Laney by any chance?"

"As a matter of fact, I have."

"Could you—."

"She's down by the lake—." She points her finger in my direction, "but you didn't hear that from me."

Strange, was it a secret? Maybe she didn't want to be found, but I wasn't sitting with her crazy family alone, I'd sorely regretted staying for dessert the night before, we'd all assumed she was exaggerating when she told us all of her family, clearly she was down playing just how weird the entire motley crew was, I'd gotten a migraine just listening to them, I thanked the only sane person in this house and headed for the lake with the directions she'd given.

The walk to the lake was a peaceful one, I could see why she liked it so much, there were hidden depths to her that I never realised or maybe I just never took the time to notice, she had hidden layers that unraveled slowly the more time you spent with her, but it was like a curse, the more time you spent with her, the more addicted to her you'd become.

Watching her from the trees, just laid by the lake, my heart very nearly stopped, she was breathtakingly beautiful, just seeing her like this, innocent and carefree, she looked like she didn't have a care in the world, I tried to look around to see the view that she loved so much, but try as I might I couldn't peel my eyes away from her, she was a vision, like she belonged here by the lake, her long hair swishing around her body like a beautiful mermaid, her slender body almost hidden by the mound of greenery she lay upon, in that moment I knew, there was definitely something about Laney, she had put my heart in my mouth, every time I'd looked at her my heart had beat so fast I'd thought it would fall out of my chest, yes Laney was an enigma, she had stole the breath from my body and if I had her attention I'd gladly give it to her.

Taking small steps towards her, I wasn't sure what my next move was, I never was sure when I was in her presence, all I knew was that she was there and I needed to be near her, kneeling before her head, her beautiful eyes are closed, reaching down, gently touching her shoulders, a small sigh leaves her lips, shit, even that small simple gesture has my cock jumping in anticipation, her eyes slowly open and she finally looks up at me, "Beau—." Moving my head down my lips crash down on top of hers, gasping all her desire into my mouth, I can feel her trembling beneath me, swiftly moving around her, my lips finally release hers, pushing my body down onto hers she gasps once more, what is it about those sweet little gasps that sends the blood rushing straight to my cock, I don't know, but every time she does it the pulsing in my pants shows the hidden desire I have for her—all for her.

"What are you doing here?"

"Would you believe me if I told you that I missed you." She shakes her head, "oh, little elf, you still don't know what you do to me do you?"

"I—I don't do anything to you."

"You can't possibly believe that." Pressing my body further into hers so she can feel my throbbing cock against her pelvis, her body jolts, but she's still quiet, gripping hold of her hand I move her hand on top of my groin so she can feel the pulsing she's created, "oh, fuck." She breathes out, finally she gets it.

"Beau—." My lips press against her neck and those sweet little moans I love hearing so much spill out of her gorgeous mouth, placing my fingers into her mouth, I'm not sure how she will react but she surprises me, she starts suckling and moaning, gagging, and slurping, a mix of saliva and slurping the deeper I push my fingers down her throat and all I can think is, fuck, she's perfect.

Sliding my hands inside her loose gray sweats I find her bare, fuck, my cock jumps, she's already soaking, her gurgling and gagging picks up pace, dipping my fingers inside her hot, sticky hole, I feel her tremble beneath my touch, shoving my fingers further down her throat her pussy clenches tight around my fingers, the moans, gurgling, gagging, spit melds with her sudden gurgling moans, she feels so fucking tight as she clenches down hard around my fingers. Fuck, I want her clenching down on my cock just like this, "pull them down." I growl, I'm desperate, I'm about to fucking explode. I need to be inside of her now, she shakily pulls them down, the throbbing between my legs has passed the point of anticipation, quickly taking my jeans down over my ass, while she's still suckling on my fingers, gently I enter her dripping pussy, as soon as I push through she clamps down hard, "oh fuck," I cry out, the way she grips my cock feels like fucking heaven. I'm not even thrusting yet and I'm so close to exploding, slowly I move within her, every movement causes her pussy to add pressure to my throbbing cock, her muffled moans as she cries onto my fingers, my hand is as soaked as her pussy and it feels amazing, just been inside of her, allowing her to cock warm me, moving faster, her gurgles turn to wet moans, thrusting deeper and deeper, I feel her squirt and splash my cock with her juices, a few more thrusts as I bury myself deep within her and a jolt of my cock, I cry out at each squirt that splashes deep inside her tight fucking hole and I see stars, collapsing at the side of her, I hold her in my embrace as we just lay there breathless looking up at the clear blue sky, the only thing that can be heard are our breathless gasps and it is the most intimate I've ever been with anyone, holding Laney, I know this is just the kind of magic that has been missing from my life.

Sixteen

A Ride With Smokey

Smokey was my majestic steed, even though he was old, he could run rings around even the youngest foal, he'd been my best friend growing up, when my grandfather had bought him for me my mother had been furious, she'd even threatened to shoot him, that was the one and only time my father had stepped up and tried to appeal to her better nature, I didn't know she had a better nature but whatever he had said to her must have worked because I was suddenly allowed to keep Smokey and not only that, the builders arrived the very next day to build a stable to home Smokey. I wasn't sure why they'd built such a large one, but money talks, it seems my father convinced my mother that having horses could be an investment but she was under strict instructions to leave Smokey out of it, which she'd hated to this day because my horse had turned out to be the fastest out of all of the horses.

I was grateful for the gift my grandfather had bestowed upon me, he'd given me much more than a pet, he'd given me a lifelong friend.

Walking back to the house with Beau's hand pressed firmly in mine, we started towards the orchard where the stables had been built, I couldn't come all the way here and not say hello to my oldest friend.

"Where are we going?" He asks.

"There's someone I want you to meet."

"Not like the rest of your family is it?"

"No, he's an old friend."

"He?" He twists his face up in horror.

"Come on, you're not jealous are you."

"Should I be,"

"Oh, definitely." I laugh, teasing him.

The meadow is beautiful as we walk across it, the sun beams down on the pale green grass, in the spring it would sprout beautiful white daisies that as a child I'd spend hours making daisy chains alone in the sun, every summer I'd make a flower crown for Smokey and call him 'King Steed,' he'd neigh at me like he understood what I was saying, well I liked to think that he understood everything I used to tell him, my secret thoughts, the happiness he'd bring me merely by just existing, animals were different to us but that doesn't mean they didn't love the same, if anything they loved more and they never asked for anything in return, only that you'd love them back.

"Are we going to see a farm boy?" He asks as we step up to the stables.

"Something like that."

Walking into the stables, hay fills my nostrils, it takes me back to a time when I'd just sit here and admire the horses, most people feared horses because of their size, but not me, to me they were like gentle giants.

"Beau, I'd like to introduce you to Smokey," I step aside so he can see who he thought he needed to be jealous of.

"It's a horse."

"He's not just any horse, only the best horse around," I hear a familiar neigh as he pops his head out to greet us.

"Hello," he lifts his arm waving at him and I can't help the fits of giggles that crawl through my body.

"What are you doing?"

"Saying hello—."

"You don't say hello like that, go pat his head and give him an apple."

"Oh, no."

"You can't tell me your afraid of horses."

"Not afraid—."

"Then what's the problem."

"Just don't feel like losing a hand today that's all."

"Now you're been ridiculous."

"Have you seen the size of it's mouth, that thing could swallow the titanic."

"So, I'm guessing you don't want to ride him."

"Do I look like I want to die today." It's quite humorous seeing Beau react this way, I don't think I've ever seen him look so terrified, I shrug, "your loss."

Opening the gate, I start getting him ready for a ride, Beau keeps a safe distance and for the first time since I've known him, he's silent, I wonder where his fear of horses comes from, he's never mentioned anything, I didn't think the dashing doctor was scared of anything but here he was keeping a keenly eye on Smokey lest his mouth open ready to swallow the titanic, or maybe even the world, who knows what was going around his head I think with a smile on my face.

Walking towards Beau while holding onto Smokey's reins guiding him out of the stables, he shoots out in front, making sure to still maintain a safe distance.

"What are you doing?"

"I'd have thought that was obvious."

"It looks like your bringing the giant outside."

"Don't let his size intimidate you."

"I'm not intimidated," he folds his hands across his chest like a petulant child.

It's so funny to me, a broad muscly man who is a doctor no less, is afraid of an old horse, I want to laugh, but his fear seems to be genuine, but he sure does look funny skipping around trying to avoid that monster that is supposedly threatening his life.

I give Beau a gentle peck on the cheek, "I will be back soon."

"Where are you going?"

"For a ride." He shakes his head, "you can't leave me here."

"Then come with me."

"On there." I nod, "you first."

"You don't want your own horse to ride?"

"I don't even want to ride this one, but your not giving me many options."

Placing my foot on the stirrup, I fling my leg around, shifting my bottom closer to Smokey's head so Beau has room to sit behind me, I motion for him to get on, he once again looks like he's doing a dance, laughing, "are you coming or not."

"Damn you, Laney." He doesn't get on the horse quite so elegantly, but he finally manages to seat himself behind me, with his hands firmly wrapped around my waist, "are you ready?" I ask.

"No." Gently nudging the side of Smokey, he starts trotting down the meadow and all I hear is a high pitched shrill scream behind me, I'm laughing that hard I very nearly fall off of the horse.

I wouldn't mind, we were going slower than an old granny crossing the road, I never realised how dramatic he could be, guess I'd found his weakness, horses.

We don't ride for too long, but on the way back, the screaming dissipates and I think maybe he's actually enjoying it, now that it's over.

"First time riding?"

"No, I do it all the time."

"I can tell, you're a pro."

"What gave it away." He laughs.

"The girlish screaming."

"I did not," he pouts.

Flapping my arms in the air, I start screaming in a high pitched tone, flailing my arms around, mimicking what I'd assumed were his moments of fear.

"Why, you—."

He jumps forward, I try dodging his fast attack, but he catches me just before I can get away, wrestling me to the ground, loud fits of giggles once again erupt from deep inside of me, crushing my body with his, his mouth comes down hard on top of mine, savoring the taste of Beau on my tongue, his mouth moves expertly against mine, once again taking my breath away, coming up for air, our lips finally part and I'm lost in the moment, just laid in the green meadow outside the stables entangled in Beau's embrace, I smile, while staring back into his crystalline ocean blue eyes that I seem to get lost in every time he holds me like this, it's like time stands still, there is just him and me.

It's a love everyone searches for, where time exists only for the two of you, the air is cold but still, we are frozen in a moment, entangled in this quite serene moment, it's where magic happens, where you suddenly believe that anything is possible because the way he's looking at me right now, if I could freeze time, I'd freeze this moment right here, to forever stay locked in his embrace.

I've had many fond memories here, the happiest, this was my happy place beyond the lake, if you'd asked me to pick a favourite memory I'd have trouble deciding, but with him right now, like this, I now know what I'd pick, in a frozen capsule I'd bottle this moment with Beau because right now, feeling the warmth as his body presses against mine, he's unknowingly created a new memory.

A memory that would last a lifetime, this moment right here is now my favorite place, not the meadow, not the stables, not even the lake, but Beau, he's my favourite place.

Seventeen

The Hunger Games

The last day at crazy Manor and it was the day I had been dreading the most, of course, my morning at the lake was made that much more appetizing once Beau had arrived, but nothing could stop the pain that was about to ensue, not even the delicious display Beau had created this morning, I hated the hunger games, not sure how this tradition had started, but every year I prayed that it would stop. If my crazy family hadn't scared Beau off already, surely this would, I'm not sure why rich people found this entertaining, it was just cruel.

"The day you've all been waiting for is finally here." My mother announces as she stands, the whole room erupts into cheer because this is probably the highlight of their vapid year.

"What's happening?" Beau whispers in my ear.

The question I'd asked myself many times over the years, I never joined in because I never brought anything to the game, but I still had to watch the monstrous game unfold and it tore away at my soul each time I'd watch.

"Laney hasn't brought anything as usual—." The entire room groans and boo's to show their disappointment, "unless you'd like to offer up Beau as your volunteer."

Offer up Beau, has she lost sense of reality? Was she really that fucking stupid? "No, I would not." I scowl.

"What is it? Maybe it will be fun." He whispers once more.

"Trust me, it's not, if you want to leave after the games—."

"Fuck, Laney why would I leave, why do you still think so little of me?"

"I don't."

"Then stop pushing me away."

"I'm not, oh what's the point, you'll see."

"See what?"

I don't answer him, after all, he'd get to see with his very own eyes just how fucked up and deranged the Powell family actually was, I was begging him to leave, not only because I was scared to be alone with him, but because I never wanted anyone to see this—especially not Beau.

One by one they walked their 'gift' to the front of the room facing the crowd, they stood there smiling, unaware of the doom that was about to befall them, over the years I'd tried to warn them, but money was the root of all evil, those that had it did stupid shit like this and wrapped it up in a pretty bow and named it 'entertainment' and those that didn't have it—well they'd do anything to get it, I suppose you could call them greedy, but if you were desperate and you had the chance to make a fool of yourself to win a cash prize at the end of it to change your life, I guess you'd do it, but not me, you couldn't pay me enough to act like a monkey for the rich and stupid, I roll my eyes as they eagerly stand there with smiles upon there faces, awaiting the challenges that they'd be given.

"The gift are people?"

"Yeah, stupid people."

"Laney, are you okay?"

"I'm fine." I mutter as my mother steps forward ready to run across the ridiculous rules of the game.

"Now, the volunteers are in place, one lucky volunteer will leave here richer than they arrived, but I will warn you, it won't be an easy task, what will you be willing to do to change your life?"

As always she turns towards the volunteers and they all cry, "anything." In unison, which seems to appease the crowd as it erupts into cheer once more.

"What happens to the losers?" Beau asks.

"Were not monsters—." I almost have to laugh because that's exactly what they are, "they have a warm meal and get sent home." She smiles.

"I don't really understand the point." He whispers.

"Join the club." I smile.

"So you've never played?" I pull a grimace, "of course you haven't little elf, that heart of yours is much too big." His words instantly send a warmth into my heart.

A tall man wearing waiter attire walks in pushing a silver trolley with seven platters for the eager contestants, one by one he places them by their feet, then walks off in the direction he's just arrived, looking at the bowls at their feet I grimace, game one is always the same and it's never not being any less disgusting the more you watch it.

"The contestants will kneel on the floor and eat every drop, you cannot use your hands, just your mouth, the contestants that finish move onto the next round."

"What is it?" One tiny scrawny looking contestant asks.

"It's kibble dear." My mother smiles, "very nutritious you know."

"Really—." I eye her, "why don't you eat it then mother."

"Laney, don't be insolent." She scolds.

"Excuse me—." One of the contestants raise their hand as if they're in school, "what is kibble."

I watch as my mother hums with this particular question knowing full well she's not going to answer them, "it's dog food." I call, hoping that at least one of them will have the decency to back out, but as silence encases the room I can see that won't happen.

"Dog food, she's making them eat dog food." I look at his shocked expression, "still time to leave." I offer, he just shakes his head, but I can't get the pitiful look he has on his face out of my head and I know what it is, it's pity for the people that are about to be treat worse than animals, all in the name of entertainment.

We look on in horror as the crowd cheers on their volunteer, on their hands and knees they dip their faces into the bowl, gagging on the food as they try gobble down every piece of kibble, two of them throw up and attempt to continue eating it, the bell rings and only five contestants remain, the other two are taken through to the kitchen to claim their hot meal before they are shipped off home.

"This is utter madness Laney, this can't be legal."

"Since when did the rich care about the law, didn't you know with enough money, you can get away with murder, plus do you see them forced to do it? They are willing participants."

"But why?"

"Money makes the world go round, I guess."

"Maybe if someone—."

"Don't bother, I've tried, all they care about is the money and all they care about is seeing their monkeys jump through their hoops for a tiny morsel of what they have, one million is pennies to these idiots."

"That's the prize?"

"Yep and they'll do anything to get it."

"Madness."

"Agreed."

I wasn't sure what was going through Beau's head right at that moment but I knew it couldn't be anything good, he looked positively horrified, but why wouldn't he, this was the stuff nightmares were made of, a cruel game to keep them entertained, but these people were beneath them, why wouldn't they treat them as puppets, after all they had something they wanted and they could have it, all they'd have to do is sell they're soul to the devil for it.

The games went on, each round more horrific than the first, Beau actually gagged when they were made to drink urine, funnily enough they all passed that round, I'm not even sure who's urine they were drinking, nobody asked and my dear sick, twisted mother never divulged any information, so they just got on with it, probably hoping this night would be over, much like myself.

We were coming close to the final round and this was where they really got inventive, you see they'd all offered input into what they would have to do round by round, they had meetings months in advance, of course I was never invited because I'd never made it a secret what I thought of their horrific games, so every year it would be a surprise even for me.

There were three contestants left standing, which was more than usual, in fact I wasn't quite sure anyone had ever won these games, you see there was a small clause in the joining of these games, you had to complete all seven rounds to be crowned winner and the last one that was still standing would go home with their cash prize.

"Now, this round will not be an easy task—." Like any of the others had, but nobody was prepared for what she was about to say next, "you will each be given pliers and you must take off a fingernail of your choice and eat it."

There were no cheers, there were no happy sounds racing through the room like there had been on the other rounds, the only thing that filled the air was deathly silence, I'd seen them do some pretty horrific things to the volunteers, but they'd never asked them to maim themselves, the shock runs across my body before the anger settles in.

"You can't be serious." I scream.

"Laney, if you can't be quiet leave."

"Gladly." I spit back at her, making a secret vow to myself to never darken her doorstep again, I mean honestly a fingernail? A fucking fingernail, how was torture classed as entertainment, I wasn't staying to watch that massacre, no fucking way.

They'd all need therapy by the time this night was over, but one of them could cry into their bag full of money, so I'm sure that would be compensation enough, after all who needs fingernails anyway, I shake my head as I storm out of the room with Beau following close behind.

"Are you okay?" He asks me when we finally reach my room.

"I'm fine—don't I look fine." I can already feel the tears stinging the back of my eyes, threatening to fall.

"No." I feel him sit beside me, his arm comes around my shoulders, I try push him away from me because I know I'm moments away from crumbling.

"I—said—I'm fine." I manage to get out, as the first tear drops down my face.

"You're not fine, princess, come here." He instantly lifts me onto his knee wrapping his arms around me as you would do a small child, allowing me to sob into his chest, my head resting against his chest I could hear the thump, thump, of his beating heart, his hands stroke my hair ever do softly, "it's okay, I've got you," he soothes.

Picking me up, he lays me down in the bed, he's going to leave, I know he's going to leave, after seeing that I wouldn't blame him, I'd leave too, after all what does have to stay for? He's just seen how pathetic my life is, he's definitely going to leave.

But he surprises me, getting in the bed, he wraps his arms around me, turning, I nestle my face into his chest once more, allowing the sound of his heart to soothe my broken heart.

I always thought once I'd got here and I'd allowed Beau into my heart that it would be him that would break my heart, but he'd surprised me, he was the only person I had found comfort and safety with, it was my family that had broken my heart and they'd left Beau to pick up the pieces, as I lay across his chest, I never expected him to, but here he was, he hadn't left, he was still here.

"You're still here." I murmur into his now wet chest from the tears that had fallen only moments ago.

"Where else would I be little elf."

"Somewhere normal."

"I'm exactly where I want to be." He kisses my head and fills my heart with warmth once more, "now sleep."

For once I don't argue, I finally allow my tired, stinging eyes to fall shut, with nothing but the sound of our mixed breathing and Beau's heartbeat, I finally feel at peace, wrapped in his embrace, I finally know what home feels like and before the world goes dark, I finally realised that I don't hate Beau, quite the opposite.

I've fallen for Beau Rivers—and I've fallen hard.

Eighteen

Back To Reality

We never speak about what happened, after all its not exactly a conversation you'd want to bring up, he looks just as I always did, like he lost a piece of his soul in that room, I shake my head at myself, I'd come out of obligation, but really maybe all I wanted was to be accepted by a family who had shunned me all of my life, why did I want their acceptance though, I knew I'd never get it, I didn't fit in with their etiquette, for a start I had a heart and they were soulless creatures that got their kicks out of others torture. I wish I'd come to this realization years ago, but I guess a little part of me was still that little girl holding out for a family that loved her, but I knew I'd never get it from them, I'd never get it here and after what I'd seen last night, why would I even want it.

"Are you ready?"

"For what?"

"I'm taking you home."

"You don't have to do that."

"I know, I want to." He smiles, god, could he be anymore perfect, where was the asshole that I'd loved to hate. I wasn't complaining but what a vast turnaround he'd made, maybe he was never an asshole, maybe it was always just easier to see him that way, that way I knew I couldn't get hurt, if I denied my feelings for him, completely shut them off, I knew that there was no way I'd be left heartbroken and disappointed, but somehow he'd managed to break down my walls and creep into my heart without me knowing, there's a fine line between love and hate and he'd crossed it long before this weekend, I just never saw it.

We don't say goodbye to anyone, after all what would we say? Thanks for the trauma, see you next year, except they wouldn't see me next year, next year I vowed to have a Christmas that didn't involve trauma, even if I was just sat with cookie dough watching cheesy movies alone, even that would be better than Christmas with the Kranks, so I just nod as he pulls my suitcase away from the room, once again rescuing me and taking me away from the place that had broken my heart.

"So, same again next year?" He asks once we're in the car.

Was he joking, a small slip of a smirk plays on his lips as he looks at the horrified look I more than likely have on my face.

"I'm joking, little elf." He smiles as he starts driving the car down the long road, watching in the rear view mirror as the Manor slowly disappears from my sight, laying my head back on the leather cushioned seats, I finally let out a breath that I didn't know I had been holding.

"So, your family are—interesting." I'm not sure if it's the tension we've both felt since last night or that we both really need to laugh, but at that exact moment, Beau says the perfect thing at the perfect moment and within moments the car is filled with something the Manor always lacked—laughter.

The car journey is long but comfortable, we stop off for some food and carry on our journey, we just chat about general life, leaving the horrifying experience where it should stay, back at the Manor, it's nightfall when Beau finally pulls outside of my apartment.

"Home, sweet home." He smiles, "see, even got you here in one piece."

"I never doubted you."

"Was that a compliment? From you? The mean elf, well I never thought I'd see the day."

"Beau—." I teasingly slap him on his shoulder, catching my hand he pulls my head towards his and catches my mouth with his, in one kiss, he completely consumes me, his soft lips touch mine as his tongue gently dips into mine, gasps fall from my lips into the depths of his mouth as he consumes me in the most erotic way.

"Would you like to come up?" I ask breathless.

"I thought you'd never ask." He smiles.

As he walks behind me, butterflies settle in my stomach, he's fucked me repeatedly over the last few days, but that's when I thought it was just a weekend fling, a moment of madness that would be over once we came back, but to my surprise he was coming home with me, it wasn't over, he was still here, why was he still here though, after what he'd seen I was sure he would run for the hills, but here he was, what did he possibly see in me, what did I really have to offer him, I couldn't think what would have kept him here, so the only conclusion I could come up with was—he must be crazy.

The moment we walk through the door, I expect it to be awkward, after all now that we were here, I had absolutely no idea what the next step was, did I offer him a drink? Sit down, watch something on Netflix? How were you supposed to act, I just didn't know, I felt so out of place, in my own apartment, in his presence I always felt inadequate, like he'd suddenly realise that this wasn't what he wanted, he'd come to his senses, but as I hear the door close behind him I realised that hasn't happened just yet.

His hands reach my waist pushing me up against the wall, leaving me breathless once more, his lips are on mine within moments, feeling my body lifted from the ground my legs inadvertently wrap around his body, like they'd always belonged there, "where's your room?" He whispers, I point to the far end of the room, the white door that has remained shut since my journey to hell had begun, that's when I realise not only is Beau in my apartment, but he's taking me to my room, shit, Beau is going into my room, my heart begins to race, I want to pinch myself because surely I must be dreaming, these kind of things didn't happen to people like me, he collapses our bodies onto the bed, feeling the soft blanket beneath me covered in Beau's embrace, he finally looks at me, "this is all I ever wanted," he breathes. This? What did he mean by this?

"I don't understand." He shakes his head at me, "you really are clueless aren't you."

Well, that's what I'd been told repeatedly over the last few months, what was it that Alisa said, oh yes, she said I was oblivious to what was in front of me, so yes, clueless, I guess I was, I just nod.

"Don't you know how much I want you? Even now?" I shake my head, "have I not shown you?"

"I thought it was just a fling." I whisper.

"Shit, Laney, you could never be a fling, you're all I've thought about for five fucking years, I want you."

"Then, take me." Breathless, I'm breathless, once again he's taken my breath away.

"Oh, little elf, you were mine a long time ago, you just didn't know it."

"Are you trying to ruin me."

"Yes, little elf—." his hands slide down my chest, "every fucking—," pulling my top away letting my breasts spill out, his hands grip the mounds on my chest, teasing my nipples between his fingers, hardening beneath his touch, "piece of you—." lowering his head he takes a nipple gently between his teeth, sliding his tongue along the edge, my back arches in response, "god, you're fucking beautiful." He breathes.

Taking my top over my head, he smiles, "you won't be needing this," hearing the zip as he pulls my jeans down, "or these," he runs his fingers across the thin material that covers my pussy, dipping his fingers roughly across the thin black material, pulling them forcefully down, "or these," he growls, sending tingles straight the crevice between my thighs, "just the way I like you, bare, open, fucking dripping," a slip of a moan slips out as I watch him remove his clothes, as he leans over me, I finally get to see his gorgeous physique as he gently lowers himself down, placing my hands across his chest to stop him, "no," he looks confused, "you don't want to?" I smile, "I do." His confusion seems to grow, "I don't understand."

Sliding my body across, so I'm no longer beneath him, gently pushing him, "you want to be on top?" I smile, "okay, naughty elf, I'm game."

A quick reversal and now I was leaning over him, my eyes dart to every delicious curve on his body, he has two little beauty spots on his chest that I hadn't noticed before, just glancing at his body has me in a trance, I think I could just look at him like this forever, "now you've got me where you want me, what will you do with me."

Leaning down starting at his chest, my lips come down, kissing and suckling down his chest, a small groan leaves his throat, "oh, that's a good start little elf," I feel his body react under my touch, sliding down his body, leaving a trail of my saliva in its wake, his groans are becoming more hoarse, I can see his excitement growing with the throbbing movement of his cock, a small smile appears on my lips before my head moves from his sight, "oh fuck, Laney, you know exactly what you're doing." Sliding my tongue across his balls, I feel him go rigid, teasing them into my mouth while popping them out and back in slowly, I feel his hand caress my hair while little groans fill the air, sliding my tongue gently up the length of his cock, feeling him throb beneath my tongue, sending light licks across his engorged mushroom head, his gasps and moans instantly become incoherent, “oh fuck, oh fuck,” is the most sense I hear from his rushed gasps of pleasure, my mouth comes down hard coating his cock with my saliva as he pushes my head further down, tightening around him, so he feels exactly like he does when my pussy clenches around him, moving slowly allowing his cock to make me gag each time I feel him hit the back of my throat, “oh fuck, oh fuck,” he calls out once more, speeding up, my head bobs up and down at great speed, tasting the delicious tang of his precum as it hits my tongue, “oh fuck, I’m so close.” He cries out, holding my head with both hands he pushes my head up, causing me to lose a grip on his thick cock, it bounces out of my mouth allowing the saliva to drip from my mouth, coating him, looking up at him in surprise, he leans down, picking me up, he throws me on the bed, reversing roles once more, but this time he doesn’t take his time as I feel his engorged head hit my center. I scream out from the sudden feeling of been filled by Beau once more, “oh, baby I’m not even half way in,” he smirks as he drives his cock deeper inside my dripping hole, “my cum belongs inside you, always inside you.” The thrusts come hard and fast, I’m clawing at his back like a deranged animal, while screaming at each thrust that plummets my pussy, “that’s right baby, you scream,” his hand comes around my throat as he thrusts deeper, banging his cock against my cervix, the pleasure is too much, it courses through me faster than lightning, once again I see stars, “Beau, I—I—it’s—too—much.” I gasp, slowing down, he thrusts gently and that's all it took, a sudden explosion erupts deep within me, splashing out at a speed I didn't even know was possible, gushing out and down my thighs, my back arches as the final pool of my pleasure subsides.

"Beau?"

"Yes princess?" He smiles at the side of me.

"You're a fucking animal."

"What can I say," he smiles, "you bring it out in me."

Pulling me closer he once again cradles me in his arms, this must be what heaven feels like, laying my head against his warm chest, listening to his fast heartbeat, I'm where I never thought I'd be, I'm home.

"Beau?"

"Hum,"

"Is this just a fling?"

"What? No."

"Then what is it?"

"Its—."

"See you can't answer, if its just sex, just tell me, because I can't do this, if you leave I don't think I'd recover—."

"This is everything I've ever wanted since I first laid eyes on you, why would I leave, you're fucking perfect—." I scoff, "do you not feel how my heart beats?" I nod, "it beats for you, and only you."

Right then and there I turn to mush, who knew Beau was romantic? Certainly not fucking me, his words clawed a place into my heart that had been waiting for him for five years, I never thought it would find him, but it turns out, he was there all along.

"Beau?"

"Yeah?"

"Did you just say you loved me?"

"Love will never be a strong enough word to express how I feel for you, you're my shining star, my light in an otherwise dark universe."

"You're my star too." I smile as his lips press gently against my head and I finally fall asleep in the arms of a man who stole my breath and breathed new life into my very existence.

My star.

Nineteen

Work Never Tasted So Good

Walking into the hospital I instantly feel paranoid, do they all know? Every corner I turn I feel like they're all staring at me, like they all know about Beau, but how could they? I was definitely paranoid.

"Hey, Laney how was your break?" Ethan is stood there smiling at me.

"Ethan, I'm going to kill you."

"Now, now, hear me out first," he has his hands up in surrender.

With my hands on my hips, I glare at him, "well, I'm waiting."

"Coffee?" He asks.

"If you're trying to sweeten me up—."

"I'm not, I just fancy a cup." Rolling my eyes, I aimlessly follow him to the canteen, awaiting his very elaborate excuse why he couldn't even tell me he'd swapped places with Beau, of course I'm glad for the mix up, but I'm not telling him that.

Sitting in the canteen I await Ethan to come back with the canteen coffee I was promised, instead he comes towards the table with Anne in tow, surprised I look up and smile, "oh, hey Anne, switching careers." She laughs at my lame attempt at a joke.

"Sorry Ethan couldn't make it, but I needed him." I smile, I couldn't believe him, he'd roped his wife into getting him out of his trick, he'd actually got her to come here this early in the morning so he didn't have to explain, my god, what a coward.

"It's fine," I offer.

"It wasn't fair for him not to let you know he couldn't make it, we both feel terrible."

"Oh, no, I shouldn't have roped him into my ridiculous plan in the first place—."

"We didn't mind, Laney, we both absolutely adore you, which is why we wanted to tell you why he couldn't come."

"Okay."

"Were pregnant." She screams, I think the entire canteen have turned their heads at this sudden outburst, the once noisy chatter has suddenly turned to silence.

"Oh-my-god, congratulations." I scream, instantly throwing my arms around Anne, "what a beautiful Christmas gift." I gush, Ethan just laughs at my very girlish display, rushing towards Ethan I bring him into a warm embrace, "does this mean I'm forgiven," looking up at him I smile, "there's nothing to forgive, it's already forgotten."

"Beau wants to see you in his office Laney." Alisa calls before she rushes back off out of sight, she was like a ghost, I mean honestly, I hadn't seen her since I'd come back and she couldn't even say hello, I roll my eyes as I walk the hall to Beau's office.

Standing outside his office I'm unsure what I'm supposed to do, do I just walk in or do I knock? I always knock, so I should knock right? It's only professional, yes I'm sure I should knock, why am I so nervous, am I shadowing him again, that's why they say to never fuck your colleagues because of situations like this, but he wasn't just a colleague—it was Beau, I shake my head at my sudden neurotic behavior and knock on his door, "come in." I hear his faint voice through the wood paneled door.

I expect him to be sat at his desk, pretending to be busy like he always did when I was summoned to his office, but as I open the door, step inside and close it, turning, there he is stood in front of me, jumping back from the sudden shock, my back bangs against the door, "finally," he moans as his mouth comes down hard on mine, his tongue dips in and out and flicks against mine causing the heat to spread between my thighs.

"Beau—." I'm breathless, "you wanted me?" He licks his lips with that wicked smile, "always."

"Very funny." I smile while swatting him on the shoulder, that wicked smile never leaves his lips, "what makes you think I'm not serious." He couldn't possibly, not here. "Beau, were at work—." His lips trail up my neck and my body trembles beneath his touch, "and, I haven't been able to get you off my mind all morning—."

Sliding my hand down the length of his body, cupping his semi-hard cock in my small hand, "I feel for you—really I do." I whisper.

"Oh, like that is it." His eyebrows raise, "afraid so, doc." pulling me by my waist towards his desk he quickly spins me around bending me gently across the desk, I can feel his now hardened cock pressing against my ass as he lays across my body, "do you still feel for me—or would rather feel me inside of you." He whispers into my back, a moan slips and that's enough for him to rag my cotton pale blue trousers down, feeling them fall to my ankles, "fuck Laney, don't you own underwear." His hands slide slowly across my pussy lips, I can hear the squelch as he moves his fingers across me, "oh, you're already ready for me, you're fucking soaking, I fucking love that." A gush of liquid pours from my center, "do you like it when I talk to you—his fingers dip into my dripping hole causing a moan to slip out, "just like this—." his fingers move further inside of me, "you're pussy wants my cock, do you feel that, your so fucking eager to cock warm me, I'm fucking throbbing for you." He ejects his hands from my pussy shoving his fingers straight into my mouth, suckling on his fingers, I taste my own desire that he's caused, "that's right baby, you taste yourself, you're fucking delicious," his cock presses against my hole pushing in, I cry out, "god, you're pussy feels so fucking good—." clenching down with his fingers still in my mouth, drool drips down onto the desk in a mix of moaning and suckling, he pushes further, my back arches as I cry out my muffled screams, "almost there, fuck you're so tight," he groans, thrusting deeper, I cry out, feeling full in both holes he thrusts his hips faster, causing my head to lay on the desk, muffling my screams with his fingers shoved so far down my throat, I'm not sure if I'm gagging or screaming, maybe a mix of both, "oh god, I've been thinking about been inside of you all morning, fuck—." he cries out as the pleasure courses through me, his words mixed with his thick cock thrusting deeper inside of me causes my pleasure to spill out coating his cock, "oh, I'm not done with you yet."

His hand grips my hair pulling my head back, his fingers slip from my lips, causing my back to arch as he manically thrusts his cock deeper inside of my swollen pussy, my legs shake as the pleasure once again hits my body, "oh fuck, Beau, yes." I scream, our mixed moaning fills the air as his cock jerks with his progressive thrusting, feeling him splash his cum deep inside of me causes me to cry out one last time, just laid across his desk allowing his trembling body to pour all of his delicious cum deep inside of my body, sweat pierces every part of my body, my hair is matted and stuck to my forehead as he finally pulls out of me, once again feeling empty, "you're insatiable,"

"Only for you, my naughty little elf." He gently places a kiss on my head.

"God, Beau—you're—."

"Yes?"

"Breathtaking." He slides my trousers back into place as he takes me in his arms, "so are you, my little star."

"Come on." My legs are still shaking from his intense passionate episode, where he just had to have me, I wasn't sure if I could even walk, "where are we going?"

"We have work to do."

"You want me to shadow you?"

"We have a few special patients that have been admitted, I'd like you to meet them."

Walking down the hall by his side, I feel his fingers brush slightly against mine and each light touch sends happy little tingles through my body, we come to a turn, **BURN UNIT** is on the side of the wall as we enter the ward, his special patients are in here? He knew since I'd lost my grandfather in a fire that I didn't come near these wards, "Uh, Beau, I can't." He holds my hand, "It's okay, I think they could use your bright smile." I shake my head, "I don't think I can."

I couldn't relive the nightmare I'd suffered as a child, my grandfather lived with us when I was only a child, he was a kind man, I used to sit with him and listen to his old war stories, he would share his custard creams with me as I heard of how he saved and helped his soldiers in his rank, he always had a multi-colored shawl that he would wrap around me as I curled up on his knee, he wasn't a very well man, his heart had deteriorated over the years and he had come to live at the Manor as he refused to go in an old peoples home, he said his final moments should be surrounded by those he loved, not strangers who only took care of him out of obligation, my mother despised his presence, he was locked away in a room where her friends couldn't see him, out of sight, out of mind, but I visited him daily.

It was a daily ritual that I'd always looked forward to, my grandfather was the only person other than Mary that had ever shown me love or kindness, but a terrible tragedy had ensued, nobody knew how the fire started, only that it had started in his room and he couldn't get out, he'd clawed at the doors and windows, screaming for help for hours, but by the time anyone knew there was even a fire, it was already too late, his body was badly burnt, he wasn't even recognizable when he'd been brought out on the trolley, the strange thing was, nobody ever knew how the fire started or how it had stayed in that one room, the day he died my world collapsed because I was back once more to being alone, the only person worth anything in my family had gone and I'd never stepped foot near a fire or a burns unit for that matter, the traumatic experience had stayed with me all these years and standing outside of this ward, my body shook with fear.

"Please, Beau—."

"Okay, but I think they'd love to meet you." Against my better judgement, I have to know, "who are they?"

"Twin girls were brought in last week, they are only ten years old." The same age I was when I lost my grandfather. "There was a malfunction with the electrics, unfortunately they lost both of their parents in a fire, they're burns are minor, but their mental state, well I really couldn't tell you, but losing both your parents, your house and all your belongings at such a young age will cause lasting damage I'd imagine, I just thought—."

"What?"

"You're good with people, Laney, I thought you could help lift their spirits—I'm sorry—I wasn't thinking."

I had a choice here, Beau was giving me a choice, I could face my demons head on and help two little girls smile, or I could live with my trauma and avoid the fire and burns unit forever, the choice wasn't an easy one, after all, it was a fire that took my grandfather away from me, when he left so did my happiness, every part of me was screaming, *'no, don't go in there'*, my body was trembling as

I relived every hauntingly horrible event that had happened that night, a sudden sadness shrouded my entire body.

"Let's do it." I force a smile, because while I didn't want to do this, I really didn't want to do this, but if I could bring those two little girls even a little comfort, they'd have something I never did, somebody who not only understood what they were going through, but somebody who cared enough to sit with them while they were in pain.

"Are you sure?"

"No, but let's do it anyway."

Walking into the room where the two girls resided, I just watched them, chatting happily, they'd lost everything and still they managed to smile, I was instantly amazed, they weren't feeling sorry for themselves and I was glad they had each other to lean on, Beau was right, they're burns were only minor, a few scars on their face and up their bare arms, my heart instantly burst just watching them, I'd seen adults who weren't as brave as these two little girls, there little blonde curls hung loosely at there shoulders, tiny little freckles adorned their little button nose and piercing green eyes that shone each time they'd look at each other, you could see the love they carried for each other.

"They're so brave." I whisper.

"Yes, they are, they remind me of someone else." I shake my head, I was nowhere near as brave as these two little girls, "what you've endured would have broke the strongest man, you my little star are made of tough stuff." I smile, "would you like to go say hello?" I nod my head and for the first time since I entered the burn unit, I give him a real genuine smile.

"Hey, Lucy and Lacey, this is a very special nurse, she'd like to say hello."

Stepping forward, I smile, "Doctor Rivers tells me that you two are the bravest patients we've ever had and I just had to meet these warriors." They instantly smile.

"You're pretty." They both meekly speak in unison.

"And you two must be princesses." They both laugh.

I spend most of the afternoon sat with the brave twins, they tell me all of their stories and when they speak of there parents, they don't speak with sadness as you'd expect, they speak about them with love, in fact as they talk about what they've lost, they smile, I make a vow to visit them again, I'm absolutely in awe of how strong they are for such a young age, Beau was wrong, there mental state was just fine, but I think he knew that when he brought me here, after all, they had each other and loving grandparents they'd be living with when they were discharged from the hospital, this wasn't about lifting there spirits, it was about lifting mine, but it really put into perspective, what I'd been afraid of wasn't the fire at all, it was the grief from losing the only family member who'd ever loved me, that I'd never dealt with.

Walking out into the hallway, I feel lighter than when I'd arrived, walking into that room helped me more than those two little girls, Beau's gesture instantly spread to my heart.

"Thank you, Beau."

"No, thank you, you really brightened—."

Jumping at him, I don't even care if we're seen, we've not told any of the staff but what he's just done for me, I could never put into words, my arms encircle around his neck, pressing my lips hard against his, he rocks back into the wall from the force of my surprise kiss, pulling his arms around my waist, he pulls me in closer, "I love you." I just stand there staring into space, I'd said it, oh-my-god, he was smiling as he bent down and kissed the tip of my nose, "I love you more, little star."

Twenty

What Do We Have Here

It's been a few months since Beau swept me off of my feet and saved me at Christmas, spring is almost arriving and every moment with Beau has been like a dream, I'd often wondered what life with Beau would be like and it was more perfect than I could ever dream up in my head, nothing could spoil it.

Rising early, I get the sudden urge as my stomach turns and bile starts making its way up my throat, "oh, not again." I groan, only just making it to the bathroom to reach all the bile from the invisible food I hadn't eaten, a knock on the door disturbs my violent reaching, "Laney?"

"Be out in a minute." I call.

Fifty minutes later and I descend the bathroom, a little weaker than when I arrived in it.

"God, you look like death."

"Thanks, Alisa, can always count on you to point out the obvious."

"Maybe, you need to see a doctor," she winks, "know any?"

"Very funny."

"It's just a bug."

"That, or—."

"Or what."

"You're pregnant." She laughs, "but that's ridiculous, I'm sure you wouldn't be stupid enough to get knocked up."

"No." I force out a laugh, "of course not." She rushes out of the door and I slump down on the settee, almost as if I'm in a trance, *' no, I couldn't possibly be, surely, it's just a bug, yes, that's it, damn Alisa and her whacky ideas, still wouldn't hurt to make sure right?'*

My hands shake as I take the thin piece of plastic out of the box, just staring at it like it's an alien, shit, I didn't want to do this alone, but it would probably be negative anyway, so what was I worried for, two minutes the box says, what it doesn't say is once you pee on the stick, that two minutes seems to last for an eternity, I try read a book, but I can't focus, I put Netflix on, but I just keep gazing at the table where the thin piece of plastic is either going to change my life completely or it will stay the same, it's funny isn't it, a piece of plastic has so much power and in those fleeting moments, you just see how different your life is going to be if the plastic says yes or in this case positive, I start biting my nails, counting down the seconds, I'm sure that's not helping but I'm at a loss of what else I'm supposed to do.

Alisa barges back in the apartment, I let out a loud girlish scream, "shit, are you trying to give me a heart attack."

"I forgot something, why are you so jumpy anyway."

"I'm not—."

"Oh-my-god, you got one, what does it say?"

"I don't know, I'm waiting."

"How long?"

"Fifty seconds." She plonks herself down beside me, "what are you doing?"

"You shouldn't have to do this alone."

"Don't you have to work?"

"You're more important." She smiles.

"Alisa, you really don't—."

"I'm staying, so if it's positive what are you going to do?"

"I don't know."

"Wow, imagine having Beau Rivers babies."

"You're not helping."

"Sorry, anyway, it's time." I just nod, "Do you want to?"

"I don't think I can." I whisper.

"Would you like me to do it?" I just nod, while watching her pick up the thin piece of plastic that has the answer to where my life is going, it's a daunting feeling, I look at her face and she gives nothing away, she should play poker, she's got the perfect game face.

"I knew it, it's just a bug." I smile, "yeah, sorry babe," a sense of disappointment falls across me, I'm not sure why because I wasn't ready to have a baby was I? But in those moments I'd actually convinced myself that I might be pregnant, but it turned out that I just caught a bug, from where, I didn't know.

"You look disappointed."

"Well—I—must be hormones."

"Yes, a baby plays havoc with those or so I'm told," I eye her, "you're pregnant Laney."

"What?"

"I said you're pregnant, see." She points to the test, two little blue lines show in the tiny window.

"I'm pregnant." I stare as if in disbelief.

"Yes, congratulations." She screams while throwing her arms around me, "I really have to go, will you be okay?" I just nod, "oh, Alisa wait up, I will come with you."

"Oh, you're going to tell the father?" She winks.

"It's only right, isn't it?" She just nods as I follow her outside, she doesn't really say anything, but she probably senses that I need time to absorb everything that has happened in such a short space of time.

Standing outside of the hospital, I know I should be entering, but I'm scared to step foot through that sliding door, I'm scared to go to Beau's office and change his entire life, I'm just scared that everything we've built over the last couple of months will be broken, but most of all I'm scared that once I say it out loud, that it becomes real, that there will actually be a tiny person growing inside of my belly.

"You coming?"

"I just need a moment." She just nods as she gives me one last hug, "good luck." She whispers before she disappears through the doors that I still haven't managed to go through.

I could spend all day here arguing with myself about whether I should do it or not, it was like ripping a band aid off, sure it hurts at first, but once it's done it's done, god, was I really referring my pregnancy to a band aid, I shake my head, but it appears my body makes the decision for me. I can feel the bile once again rising up my throat, ready to come out, racing through the doors, I run down the corridor colliding into the ladies, quickly entering a cubicle to once again throw up a whole bowl of nothing, wasn't you only supposed to get sick in the morning? It was almost lunchtime and here I was throwing up what appeared to be my stomach lining.

Walking out of the cubicle once again I feel weak, gripping hold of the side of the sink, my feet wobble, as my head spins, raising my head, I see Alisa wasn't making a joke, I did look like death, I'd gone a ghastly gray, running the tap I splash cold water across my face, it eases the dizziness only slightly but does nothing for the lack of color in my face, taking a few deep breaths, I ready myself to take the walk to Beau's office.

Standing outside his door, I just stare at it, I know I need to go in, but I'm terrified of the response I will get from him, he loved me when it was easy and fun, but would he love me now it was complicated? I didn't know, all I knew was the answer was on the other side of that door, the longer I stood out here, the more scared I'd get and I knew if I didn't go in, I'd never tell him, but he'd notice eventually, so it had to be today, it had to be now.

Walking into his office, it is not the scene I expect to see, a tall blonde is leaning over him smiling, looking at something, it's innocent I tell myself, but as her hand rests on his shoulder I know that's a lie, he's smiling right back at her, instantly my heart drops to the floor, he finally raises his head, "Laney." He smiles right at me, wow, he had a nerve, was this so I didn't think I saw what I just saw moments before he'd looked at me.

"Really, Beau."

"What?" He looks at me with innocence.

"Nothing, this is my fault, you—never mind."

"wait, Laney." I hear him calling me, but I don't wait, I'd thought this time was different, I'd thought he'd meant everything he'd said to me, I'd thought that everything we'd experienced together was real, but it was all a lie, I think as I run out of the hospital. I can hear his footsteps behind me, I even hear him calling me, but I never look back as the tears quietly fall down my face, I only stop running when I reach my apartment, collapsing against my door I finally let the weakness and sadness crawl through my body, sliding down the door with my knees pulled tightly towards my chest, I sob. I knew if this ever happened it would break me because, damn him, I'd fallen for him, I'd fallen hard, on top of that, I was carrying his baby and while I was getting up the courage to tell him, he was busy flirting with my replacement.

I spend the rest of the day feeling sorry for myself in bed, I half expect him to come knocking at the door, but that's not realistic, he has to work, he can't leave just because he was caught and why would he, he has Blondie to keep him company, I'm sure she will fill my place faster than it took me to leave him.

"So, how did it go?" Looking up through my tear stained eyes, "What do you think?"

"I don't understand."

"He was with another woman." She shakes her head, "He wouldn't—."

"Oh but he did."

"But that makes no sense."

"That's who Beau is."

"He's been chasing you for years Laney, everyone knows that, that's why women would throw themselves at him, but he nev- er—."

"Well, I guess one did."

"Bastard." I smile, "you eaten yet?"

"No."

"How about we order take out and watch rubbish on television, hey, I can even run to Joe's and get you that cookie dough you love so much."

"You don't have to do that."

"What else would I do?"

"I don't know, go have fun, instead of babysitting your pathetic roommate."

"Hey, you're not pathetic and I couldn't think of anything else I'd rather do."

That's exactly what we did, we didn't mention Beau once, only with strict instructions she was to tell him nothing about me, he'd lost that right the day he thought he could get away with whatever that was that I'd witnessed in his office earlier, it was nice to just forget about Beau even for a little while, to just pretend that my life hadn't just been ripped apart, that I was now a nurse in a dingy apartment who was going to be a single mother and I'd have to look for another job. I couldn't continue working with him, a reminder of the one thing that had broken my heart, he'd given me so much peace and happiness, crawled into my heart and soul, I'm not sure why he wouldn't just break up with me if he'd suddenly decided I wasn't what he'd wanted, in one day I'd lost everything that had made me so happy, but I'd also gained something precious, I'd gained someone who needed me more than my heartbreak.

Alisa was falling to sleep, so I'd sent her to bed, she'd have probably stayed up all night with me if I'd have asked, but that would be unfair to her, she'd be dead on her feet when her shift came tomorrow and it would be all my fault, all because I didn't want to be alone, no, that most definitely wasn't fair. Beau had repeatedly rang my phone, to which I'd not answered, he would just try talk his way out of it, it was best we had no contact at all, it was just cruel of him to keep popping up like that after he'd broke my heart, it was expected though. I knew once his shift was over he'd try calling, I'd half expected him to show up, at least he had the decency to understand that I genuinely didn't want to speak to him, maybe I would one day, but not today.

When Alisa had to go to bed, that's when when I really got a sense of what my life would be like, I'd stupidly made Beau my entire world and now that he was gone, I felt, I don't know, empty. I felt lost without him, but if I just swept it under the carpet, it would give him a free pass to do it again and men who do it once, will always do it again, it's best to just chalk it down to a fling and move on, but he wasn't a fling, I'd fallen in love with him, he'd broken my heart once again and I had unknowingly let him, how could I be so stupid. I should never have started this thing with Beau, right from the beginning I had known it would end in my heartbreak, but on some level, I guess I just hoped that this time, this time would be different, but he'd shown me what I knew all along, that a leopard couldn't change it's spots, he was who he was and I was who I was and nothing could change that, no matter how many times you wished it could.

Maybe he'd felt trapped and he didn't know how to tell me that this isn't what he'd actually wanted, maybe he'd got cold feet, maybe he was going to tell me, but once again I'd caught him in the act, there were so many things I just didn't know. I didn't know how he could look so innocent while he looked at me, he must have known how I'd react, I'd gave him an out months ago and he'd said it wasn't a fling, maybe it wasn't, maybe he had wanted more, but temptation was something he didn't seem to know how to control. I'd only had Beau for a short time, but in that short time, I thought I'd finally found my happy ever after, I thought this was it, the one I'd spend the rest of my life with but as I lay my head on my fluffy pillow that gives me some semblance of comfort, I realised I didn't find my happy place after all, I'd just experienced fleeting moments of what I thought could have been a happy end to my already traumatic existence.

How can you go from being blissfully happy one moment and then having your whole world ripped apart. I'd never felt sadness like this before, could you die from a broken heart? It felt like my heart had been ripped from my chest, could you go on without a heart? I wasn't sure, but as I'd already gave mine to him, I hoped that it was the latter, he was supposed to handle my heart with care, I'd never gave my heart to anyone, but with Beau, I'd have gave him my last breath if he'd have asked, I gave him every piece of me and now I was broken, broken from the heart that lay missing in my beating chest. My heart had felt so much warmth, it almost had burst, but now as I close my eyes, it felt empty and the only thing I felt in my chest was pain and sorrow as I allowed the pain to flow through my chest and fall into tears down my face.

I was lost, then he'd found me, I was broken and he'd healed me, when he was gone he took the warmth, happiness and light right out of my life and I was left in a sobbing mess in the dark for the lost love I'd forever mourn.

Twenty-One

I Need This—For Me

I'd spent the last few days crying and moping around, I'd took a leave of absence, I couldn't face seeing anyone, least of all Beau, Alisa had tried comforting me and when she was around I'd put on a brave face, but I knew I wasn't really fooling her, after all how could I, my eyes were puffy and red everyday. I wasn't sure if it was my hormones that made me cry so profusely or the fact that I'd let him in, against my better judgement, I'd let him in, even though I knew it wouldn't end well.

It was almost laughable that he'd thought flowers would repair everything, had to hand it to him though, he'd really stepped up to the heartbroken act, everyday flowers would arrive, roses, tulips, every flower arrangement was beautiful, each with a hand written card begging me to speak to him, how was I supposed to forget about him if all he did was send me daily reminders of him, was that his game, to torture me death! Of course, I'd thought about tearing them into little pieces like he'd tore at my heart, but looking at them, I just couldn't do it. I couldn't keep them either, so the only sensible option was to send them right back, with a blank card, he didn't deserve even my written words, he'd get nothing from me. I'd hoped he'd get the message that I really didn't want to speak to him, that all I wanted was to be left alone, but the stubborn bastard didn't let up, everyday more flowers would come.

"Another delivery." Alisa calls.

"Send them back."

"Laney, how long are two going to play this game?"

"Until he gets the message."

"I don't think that's happening anytime soon."

I hated to say it, but she was right, he would continue to send them until he got his own way, if it was up to him, I'd be covered in bloody flowers. I knew what he was doing, he was trying to charm me until I gave in, but I wasn't going to give in, I just wanted peace, I'd left him alone, why couldn't he do the same for me.

"Why don't you just hear him out?"

Had she not listened to a word I'd said over the last few days, had she not seen how much it had broken me to walk into that office and see him with another woman, and her great answer was to hear him out, the one thing I'd avoided since that day, what made her think he had anything to say that I'd want to hear, the only thing that Beau was good at doing and that was lying. I wasn't waiting around to hear him out, I'd only be left disappointed anyway, so why try.

"No."

"What's the plan then?"

"What do you mean?"

"You can't avoid him forever, you work at the same hospital."

"I'm not going back."

"Okay, work aside, what about the flower explosion that arrives everyday?"

"I don't know."

"I mean it's not like you can go to another country." She jokes, my eyes widen.

"What a great idea."

"Laney, I was joking, you can't move to another country." She screams.

"Not move."

"What then?"

"Just visit." She shakes her head, "I need a break."

"So, go to the beach."

"I think I need to do this."

"You can't go alone."

"I will be fine, hey, maybe I will come back a new woman." I smile.

"I was joking, though."

"Your a genius." I smile, while wrapping my jacket around my body.

"Where are you going?"

"I have a holiday to book." I smile.

"Wait—Laney." She calls, but I know she's just going to convince me why I shouldn't go, but over the last few days of heartbreak and misery, it seems to be the only thing that makes sense right now, after all, why shouldn't I go, what was keeping me here—nothing, sun, beach and a refreshed perspective here I come, hopefully.

I had a doctors appointment, they had confirmed my pregnancy and I needed to have my first official meeting with my midwife, it wasn't as scary as I'd thought, but what did I know, everything from hear on out was new, I had gotten the all clear from the midwife to fly, so all I needed to do was book a flight, my only issue was, I didn't know where I wanted to go. I'd never thought about going on holiday, it was just never something that had crossed my mind, however, I suppose I had never been put in a position where I wanted to escape my life.

That's what women usually did in movies wasn't it? They'd go on holiday to find themselves, find there happy place, go out in search of there soul, ironically they'd usually find a man, like that was supposed to be the end game all along, but my story would be different. I wouldn't be searching for a man, I'd be searching for myself, **'Laney's Great Adventure,'** it had a ring to it, yes that's what I'd name my trip, it's impulsive and out of the blue, after all what is life for if not for living and I hadn't been living lately, well, maybe a living corpse.

I'd been acting like I'd died, I'd given up on not only myself, but life and that I wasn't okay with, sure I'd had my heartbroken, but at least I'd felt love in order for it to break and now I was looking for a different kind of love, I was looking to fall back in love with myself. I'd never had a great relationship with myself, I'd abused the girl I was, not taken notice of her needs, never let her use her voice even when she was screaming at me, the relationship with myself was going to be my most important one yet, I'd find the girl who I was supposed to be, show her that even when life knocks you down, you get right back up, yes, I was ready to give love to Laney Powell.

After all she'd spent far too long in the dark, the love I'd been searching for was there all along, I thought it had to come from another person, but what I didn't see, is it had to come from me, within me, the only person that could fix me, was me, and I was ready to love myself so strongly that life would be my next great adventure because life was a gift, my story hadn't ended because I wasn't willing to give up on life, after all it hadn't given up on me, walking into the travel agents I smile, ready to embark on my next great adventure.

Walking into the travel agents, beaches and getaways adorn the walls, looking at the clear sandy beaches makes me instantly smile, the room is light and airy with a vague scent of vanilla that fills the air, everywhere you look there are smiling people, after all, why wouldn't they be smiling, they're booking a getaway, it certainly made me smile, sitting down on the plush seats in the seating area, picking up a travel brochure, flicking through, secretly hoping that something will pop out at me because I still have no clue where I'd like to go. Maybe I wasn't the only one who came here clueless, surely I wasn't the only person in the world that didn't know where there destination was, after all people go in search for themselves all the time, flicking through the pages my eyes land on something that intrigues me, backpacking through Europe, that looks interesting, but probably not the best thing to do when you're pregnant, now I was back to square one, why didn't they have a big ball that you could spin, like on the lottery and a destination of your choice pops out, that would solve all my indecisive decisions.

"Can I help you?" A tall, red headed woman approaches me, in her navy blue attire and her kind smile, I instantly warm to her welcome.

"I want to book a holiday."

"Right this way."

Sitting down, a little more nervous than when I'd arrived, I just sit there silently as I watch her type away, it was a little unnerving just sat here, after all I was about to make a huge leap and there she was just typing away with not a care in the world at my internal struggle, but I couldn't blame her for that, after all she didn't know my situation.

"Where would you like to go?" She smiles, well, that was the question of all questions, where would I like to go. I just stare at her blankly because try as I might, I can't think of anywhere that

I'd put on my bucket list that I wanted to go visit, I know people usually made a list of all the places they wanted to see before they died, but I never created one because travel was never on my list of things to do.

"Honestly, I don't know."

"That narrows it down," she laughs.

"Do you do surprise destinations by any chance." It was a long shot, I wasn't even sure that was a thing, after all who would get on a plane knowing they had no idea where they'd land—me it appears.

"Actually, we do."

"Perfect."

"When would you like to go?"

"Today."

She starts manically tapping on her keyboard tutting to herself, with some slight moans and groans dropping from her mouth, I was eagerly waiting to find out if I was going to be heading on my surprise adventure.

"I'm afraid not," it appeared that my adventure would have to wait, "but we do have a spot open for tomorrow if that works," I smile and nod as she hashes out the details for my surprise getaway.

I was in good spirits when I left the travel agents, it was the middle of the afternoon and I felt like treating myself, well apart from the lavish holiday I'd just treated myself to, but that was different, I spotted a quaint little cafe on the corner, wouldn't hurt to stop in for a warm drink, I think to myself.

The warmth instantly hits me as soon as I walk in the cafe, cute little tables are nestled around with quaint little cushioned crimson seats, the lighting is low creating a romantic ambiance, soft music plays low in the background, but that's nothing compared to the delicious aromas now attacking my nostrils, my belly rumbles just from the intoxicating smells of fresh coffee beans and bacon, my mouth almost waters as I make my way towards the counter, ordering a malted mocha latte and one of those appetizing bacon baps. I stand waiting for the delicacy that I can't wait to demolish, a small tap on my shoulder takes me out of the trance of all the hidden smells that keep hitting me, turning I smile.

"Ethan," I scream as I throw my arms around his neck.

"Hey, stranger want to come sit,"

"Oh, I have to wait—."

"We will bring it over to you doll," the waitress intersects, great I think, thanks for nothing.

Once seated, Ethan doesn't give me time to breathe before he's flying questions at me left, right and center.

"You don't look sick."

"Oh, no I am," I try fake cough.

"Is this about Beau?"

"Why would it be."

"Every one knows you two had a thing."

"Well, everyone should mind their own business."

"He's miserable you know."

"I don't care, I don't want to talk about Beau." He looks sad, "hows Anne?"

"She's doing good Laney, but she's worried about you."

"Tell her she doesn't need to."

"Were all worried about you."

"I'm fine."

"Won't you at least talk to him?"

"No."

"Well, what did he do?"

"Ask him that."

"I did, he doesn't know."

The kind waitress interrupts at the perfect moment, I came here for a treat, not to run into Ethan who's main topic of the day was Beau. I was sick of having the same conversation with everyone, Alisa was the same, evidently Beau was back to being a martyr and I was just the hateful bitch.

"Yes, we all know Beau is perfect—."

"I'm not saying that."

"No, well what are you saying."

"Maybe, you're overreacting."

Overreacting? Was he joking? After everything how did I become the head case and Beau still came up smelling of fucking roses, he couldn't force me to speak to him, anymore than he could force me to sit here and listen to this crap, I thought Ethan was my friend but every time it involved Beau, Beau would win, so maybe he was actually more Beau's friend than he was mine.

"Yeah, maybe your right, maybe I walked in on Beau with another woman in his office, maybe he acted like I hadn't seen anything, then maybe he broke my fucking heart."

"Laney, I didn't—."

"Yeah, well maybe if you didn't believe every lie he told you, you'd have asked me."

Picking up my hot drink and sandwich, I stand because thanks to Ethan this pretty quaint cafe had suddenly lost its appeal, he puts his hand gently on my wrist, "please don't leave like this Laney."

"Just tell Beau to leave me alone, its over."

Walking away, I turn to look back and Ethan had his head down, I don't know why, it's not like I'd just broken up with him, why was he so sad.

Walking back to my apartment with my shoulders slumped down, I suddenly feel a wave of sadness wash across my body. I hadn't said those words out loud until today, I hadn't even thought those words, saying them out loud seemed so final. I mean clearly I knew it was over, but as I said those words they had hung in the air and followed me home like a black cloud had been placed above my head and I was back to the heart wrenching depression I'd been stuck in since it happened, why couldn't he just say hello like a normal person, no he had to get on his high horse about Beau. I wasn't happy that he was miserable in fact that made me feel worse, after all, I didn't need to know that, but somewhere deep inside of me, I felt like he deserved it after all he'd brought it on himself.

After I've eaten and drank my treat that now doesn't feel like a treat, more like a reminder of my disaster run-in with Ethan, I half contemplate just sitting in my depression right where I was before I'd decided to get away, I'd been some semblance of happy before Ethan had turned my smile upside down, the tears fall down my face and this time I let them, as I pack my suitcase ready for my adventure, yes, I'd allow my sadness in one last time, because a breakup was like grief, one day the tears would stop, one day I'd stop mourning him, one day I wouldn't think him as much as I do now, one day everything would be better. I'd be better, until that day came I'd pretend that I was happy, I'd pretend with all my heart because one day, I would.

One day it wouldn't hurt as much, I knew I'd love Beau until my dying breath, I always had and I always would, what happened between us would never change that, after all in such a short space of time he'd given me so many happy memories, it's funny isn't it how you can have a million memories with someone and if they do something to hurt you or break your heart, that's the final memory your left with and all those wonderful times just slowly disintegrate and one day my sad memory of Beau would disintegrate too and then I'd finally be able to keep him close to my chest, in my heart, where he'd stay forever.

But that day wasn't today, I was mad and damn it I'd earned the right to be mad and nobody was taking that away from me, I wouldn't always be mad, but today I was, or maybe I wasn't, maybe I was just—sad.

Twenty-Two

Don't Be Mad, Be Happy

I couldn't believe Ethan, I knew as soon as I'd seen him that I'd regret walking into that cafe, but the smells had intoxicated me, I'd never expected that, not from Ethan, he was supposed to be my friend, although he hadn't been much of a friend lately, so I shouldn't be so surprised, but the fact he blamed me for Beau's misery was one thing I wasn't standing for, if Beau was miserable it was from his own doing, not mine, not anyone else's but his own, he had to take responsibility for his own actions and realize that every action has a consequence, let him live with his, I was having to live with mine.

He'd made me so mad, the way he'd flung around his accusations, never bothering to find out what actually happened between Beau and I because evidently, Beau hadn't a clue, trust him to play the dumb injured party, I was so sick of everyone telling me to talk to him, what if I didn't want to talk to him, did they ever think of that? No of course not because the only person that mattered here was Beau, well I was sick of doing what everyone wanted me to do, I was sick of been a rug that everyone wiped their feet on, sick of people telling me what I should and shouldn't do, I wasn't a doormat and I sure as hell wasn't talking to Beau.

A knock at the door rouses me from my incessant thoughts, sneaking up to it, peeping through the little hole to see who has decided to disturb my peace, I Inwardly groan, did I want round two? Evidently I did, as I fling the door open to greet my unwanted guest, "what do you want." I scowl.

"Nice way to greet people, Laney your people skills are top notch."

"What do you want Ethan."

"Well I'd like to come in, or would you prefer to shout at me on the doorstep," he puts his hand to his mouth dramatically, "oh my, what would the neighbors think." I roll my eyes while stepping aside.

"Want to tell me what that was about?" I shrug my shoulders, "come on, Lane, I'm not the enemy here."

"Aren't you."

"No, I'm your friend."

"Sure didn't sound like it." I mumble.

"I'm stuck in the middle here, your miserable, Beau's miserable, the reason your both miserable is because your apart, it just seemed like the only plausible solution."

"Beau will get over it."

"I don't think so, I've never seen him like this."

"So he's suffering."

"Yes."

"Good."

"Laney—."

"No, he only has himself to blame and then I have you and Alisa breathing down my neck trying to convince me to talk to him, I don't want to talk to him."

"We are just worried about you."

"You don't need to be—I'm fine." My voice is shaky and I can feel the lump forming in my throat, oh no, not now, don't cry now, not in front of Ethan, I beg myself.

It's too late, no amount of internal begging can stop the tears from falling down my face, I'm not even sure why I'm crying this time, but just the mention of his name reopens the flood gates and once I start, I can't manage to stop. I feel him pull me into his body, patting my back and making soothing noises as I just cry all my frustration out on Ethan's shoulder, hey, what did you know, even after my epic meltdown Ethan was here to comfort me, turns out he was a good friend after all.

I'm not sure how long he holds me like this for, but he waits until the loud sobbing dies down before he pulls away, men don't usually deal with emotions very well, but Ethan has always been good at sensing what needs to be done in these kinds of situations, "I'm sorry," I sob.

"Hey, you've nothing to be sorry for, your in pain, anyone with half a brain can see that, I hate seeing you like this, if I could wave a magic wand and make all of your pain go away, I would."

"I know."

"I don't know how to help you Lane, I don't know how to help either of you."

That's the thing though isn't it, he can't help me, I need to feel everything I'm feeling right now, so it doesn't eat me up later. I know how bad I'm feeling, it almost feels like I'm dying—almost, but I'm not, I'm just sad, but sadness can't last forever—I hope.

"You are helping right now." I smile.

"I am?"

"Sure, just by being you."

"Laney Powell, has anyone ever told you, you can be a soppy duck sometimes." He smiles while poking the end of my nose with his fingertip.

"I have my moments." I smile.

At least I'd been upgraded to soppy from bitch, although I wasn't sure that was an upgrade. I let Ethan hold me as I cuddled close to him on the settee for the next few hours, not many people would have come to check on you after an outburst like that, but Ethan wasn't many people, he was the exception to the rule. I found comfort laying my head against Ethan's chest, it didn't matter that we just sat here in silence just like this, the fact that he was here warmed my heart. I was lucky really, not many people had people like, Ethan and Alisa, I'd struck gold with these two and I was grateful to still have them in my life.

I wanted to tell Ethan about the baby, I knew he'd be so happy for me, but with how close he was to Beau, I just couldn't risk it, if I'd thought Beau was annoying with his daily deliveries, once he'd found out I was carrying his child he'd be so much worse, probably try make a grand gesture and I could not live in a broken home with someone who didn't really see a life with me, he'd do it out of obligation, I couldn't do that to my unborn child, live a lie, live a fantasy, if I was going to share a home with anyone, it would be with someone who wanted to be there, not someone who felt they had to be there.

No, for me, for now, it the right choice keeping this secret, tucked in my womb, I'd tell Beau one day, when I was a little less angry and if he wanted to be involved I'd let him, after all, he was the father, but right now, I knew I'd crumble if I saw him. I'd be setting myself up for more heartbreak, so for now, it was just a secret I'd keep. I knew Alisa would never tell and Ethan probably wouldn't intentionally, but he loved both of us and he may think it cruel of me to keep this so close to my chest, but right now, I just wasn't ready.

"I don't want to leave you like this, but I need to get back."

"It's fine, you've done more than you think."

"So, we're okay?"

"You and I are just fine, I'm not sure anyone could fall out with a face like that." I pinch his cheeks and watch as a warm smile appears on his face.

"If you need anything, and I mean anything, call, I will be right here." I nod as I lean into his embrace, "take care of yourself, little bug." I smile as I watch him leave.

I was glad he came round, in some weird way he'd actually comforted me more than I'd care to tell him, sometimes, in the dark, when life feels hopeless, you can find the light in the people around you, sometimes when you're sad, all you really need is a friend, someone who cares enough to sense that you need them, they don't even need to say anything, but just by sitting with you, even in silence, your faith in love can return, it doesn't matter that they weren't the one to break your heart, but maybe they're the ones that are there to help you fill in the cracks.

Ethan had an energy that you just fell in love with, Beau could learn a lot from him, not that he ever would. I had no doubt in my mind that Ethan would make an amazing dad once Anne gave birth to their baby, we could have been pregnant buddies, but my situation was a tad bit more complicated than there's.

Ethan didn't know it, but by coming round to check on me, even after I had been unnecessarily aggressive towards him, he'd restored my faith in humanity, but that's all it took, one person to show you kindness when you'd hit rock bottom, to show you that not every person would treat you as bad as the person who broke your heart, he gave me a valuable tip I think I'd forget since this whole thing had happened with Beau, he reminded me that I'm important, I matter and most of all, I'm loved.

I wasn't really angry at Beau, how could I be, I still loved Beau, I was angry at myself and Ethan had helped me release part of that anger just by taking the time to be here, he knew I needed a friend and he had been there when I'd needed one the most, he'd gave me something I could never repay him for.

He'd given me hope.

Hope is what I'd lacked, hope is what I'd never thought I'd find, but I had hope now, hope that tomorrow would be different, hope that tomorrow would be less sad, hope that I'd heal what was broken inside of me and now I was certain, as long as I kept that hope I knew my sadness would be less and I'd carry that hope with me tomorrow when I embarked on my greatest adventure, it's like he knew I was leaving, but how could he? His last words felt so final, it's as if he was saying goodbye.

Goodbyes aren't forever, I'd be back, hopefully with a brand new perspective and a positive mindset, but until then I'd hope for a better tomorrow.

Twenty-Three

What Happened To Laney

Shit, where was Laney?

She hadn't been to work for days and Alisa was no help, she'd got the wrong idea when she'd barged into my office that day, but she hadn't stuck around to hear me out, she'd looked different, but now she'd disappeared from my life, it felt empty. I'd begged Alisa to tell me but I'd gotten the same response, "I'm under strict instructions to tell doctor douche nothing," great, I'm glad that nickname had resurfaced, god damn it, I hadn't done anything, this time, I hadn't done nothing.

She had ignored all of my calls, I'd sent flowers repeatedly for days, what had she done, sent them right back, if that wasn't a slap in the face I didn't know what was, she'd probably thought they were sorry flowers, forgive me flowers, that's what men did right, but that's not what they were, they were fucking talk to me and stop acting like a child flowers.

Ethan hadn't seen Laney, nobody knew when she was coming back, only that she'd taken a leave of absence due to health issues, she didn't have health issues, couldn't she come up with a better excuse than that, no, the only person who could shed light on this sorry mess was Alisa and she had refused to speak to me, not sure why because I hadn't done anything.

Why would I have smiled at her when she'd entered my office if I was up to whatever her crazy brain had come up with, but that was it, Laney didn't trust me, even now, she still saw me as the playboy that I never was, her biased opinion of me was wrong, hadn't I proved how crazy about her I was, hadn't I proved that my heart belonged to her and only her, evidently not, it was driving me crazy not being able to see her, to hold her, to touch her, was she as miserable as I was. I didn't come this far to be parted from the girl who stole my heart years ago, she couldn't just storm off and erase me from her life over a misunderstanding.

My days seemed longer without her around, come to think of it, for the last five years she'd always been there, in the background, I can't remember a time when she wasn't there, sure she'd scowl and give me her sly comments or remarks but she'd always been there and now she was just gone, the emptiness just filled me, working I felt like I was in a trance. I was here but I wasn't really partaking, it's like I was watching myself do the day to day grind, but I wasn't really here, not really and when she disappeared it really made me understand what a big part of my life she'd become.

It was only when she disappeared and stopped all communication that I realised how much I actually needed her, it wasn't a want, it was a need. I needed my star back, if she actually understood how happy she had made me then she'd have never left, I was sure of it, I never understood why she thought I just wanted a fling with her, once I'd tasted her soul, I wanted to taste her forever, with Laney it was never going to be a fleeting moment, she wasn't some rebound or girl for the weekend, she was **'the girl,'** you know the girl that puts your heart in your mouth, makes your heartbeat so fast you think it's going to stop at any moment, the one you look up at with wonder and think how did I get so lucky, what on earth does she see in me, the girl that makes your head spin faster and faster like your on a never ending roller coaster that just won't stop, yeah that girl, that's what Laney was, **'the girl.'**

Sitting in the canteen blowing on my coffee just thinking of all the things I could have done to stop her from walking away, thinking if I could go back to that day and do it over I would. I'd never felt sadness like this before, I felt completely alone, even in a room full of people, I felt deserted, the world just didn't make sense without her here.

Then I see her.

I suppose I could stay over here mulling over what I could have done differently. I could even wallow in self pity, act like I'm going to drink this cup of coffee that I actually have no interest in, or I can go over there and get some answers, fix what had broken, how many times had I tried fix it over the last few days, I'd never go to these lengths for anyone, only her, what did I have to lose?

She'd already shunned me, cut off contact, the only thing I'd hurt here is my pride and right now, that I didn't give a shit about, the only thing I cared about was Laney, getting her back where she belonged, in my waiting arms, after all there she was, a few feet away from me, she wouldn't make a scene not in front of all these people, that wasn't her style. I wasn't leaving until I got some answers, god damn it, I'd been punished enough considering I hadn't done anything and I wasn't leaving until she gave me what I wanted.

Walking towards her with my head held high, I stand next to her and she doesn't even acknowledge my presence but I know she knows I'm here from the way her body stiffens, tapping my foot on the cream tiles, she finally looks up.

"You look like shit."

"Alisa, you know why I'm here."

"I do, but I've already told you—."

"God, damn it, just tell me where she is."

"She doesn't want to see you."

"I don't care."

"Yeah, that's what got you into this mess in the first place."

"I didn't do anything."

"That's not what Laney says."

"Laney didn't stick around long enough to find out." I grit.

"I'm sorry, I can't help you."

"Yes, you can."

"Fine, I won't help you."

She won't help me, oh but she would, I'd be seeing Laney today no matter what it took. I did admire her commitment to Laney, but that commitment was the very reason why I hadn't seen her yet.

"Then you and I will have a very boring drawn out day because I'm not leaving without answers and neither are you." I hear her huff.

"Beau, come on."

"Am I not making myself clear?"

"Why don't you just leave her alone."

"I can't."

"Yes you can, its easy, stop hounding me and get on with your life."

My fist comes crashing down on top of the table, Alisa jumps and screams, the entire canteen is suddenly silent as the nurses and doctors make there way out of the canteen, probably don't want to be in the same room as the unhinged doctor who tried to put his fist through a metal table, the throbbing in my hand let's me know I hit it harder than I'd intended to.

"Jesus Beau, what the hell is wrong with you?" Sitting down I place my hands in my head.

"I can't function without her, I need to tell her that what she saw was a misunderstanding, I need her back."

"Oh shit." I look up at her, "you're in love with her."

"Yes, I've loved her for five years, I can't lose her, Alisa, I'm begging you, I just need to speak to her."

"Oh, erm—."

"What?"

"That might be a bit hard."

"Why?"

"I don't really know how to say this."

"Oh god, has something happened."

"She was so heartbroken, she cried everyday, I tried to console her but nothing I tried helped, everyday it just got worse and—."

"What the fuck happened?"

"Well that's what I'm trying to tell you."

"Well spit it out." I was becoming more agitated by the second, she couldn't even imagine the horrible thoughts that were running through my head, oh god, if something had happened to her I don't know how I'd be able to live with myself.

"She's gone Beau."

"Gone?" She just nods, "gone where?"

"Well I don't know exactly."

It was like banging your head against a fucking brick wall, in fact I think that would be preferable to this dry conversation, she wasn't making any sense, how could she be gone? And why wouldn't she know where she'd gone to and the big question still remained, why wouldn't she have told me she was going somewhere, especially when she wasn't thinking straight and she'd what just allowed her to disappear, my sadness instantly turns to rage.

"She said she needed time to think."

"Okay?"

"I'm sorry Beau, I know I should have told you, but Laney's my friend, I was just trying to help."

"Alisa, where is she?"

"She went to the airport."

"Why would she—."

"I just told you, she needs to think."

"Where is she going?"

"I swear I don't know, if you're quick, you might still catch her."

Shit, she was running off to another country to think? Why couldn't she be normal and just think, change her hair, do that dumb shit that women usually do, no, she had to travel to another country, how could she leave like this, my heart was in physical pain. I don't even say thank you to Alisa as I storm out of the canteen, my goal was to get answers but I never thought she'd run off to another country, and the worst part was, I didn't know what bloody country she was running off to.

Only moments ago, I was worried that I'd never speak to her again, but it seemed I had bigger things to worry about, if she got on that plane, then I may never see her again. I wasn't sure how I'd find her with no destination, after all the airport was a big place, it would be like looking for a needle in a haystack, I can't believe she'd do this, she hadn't even spoken to me before she had made this life changing decision, she couldn't just get on a plane on a whim.

Alisa's words ring in my head, she'd cried every night, I felt so sad, it was because of me why she was so sad because she'd thought I'd hurt her, she'd cried because she'd left me, I made her feel like she had no choice, the pain spreads to my chest, I just want to hold her in my arms and never let her go, but if I don't reach her on time, I may never hold her again.

She must have felt so low, so sad, she must have felt like she'd been left with no choice when she'd decided to leave. I hadn't helped, why didn't I just go see her, what did I think flowers and a few phone calls were going to do.

I could have fixed this days ago, if I wasn't so scared of rejection she'd never be getting on that plane today, but I was, I was scared she'd reject me, it terrified me, I was still scared she'd reject me, but stopping her from leaving before she heard what I needed to tell her far outweighed my silly fears of rejection.

I would search every corner of the world until I found her because this was not how our story ended.

It couldn't be.

Twenty-Four

Race Against The Clock

I couldn't believe she would leave like this, I knew she was mad, but shit, leaving the country just to get away from me, she must have been really mad, but what I didn't understand was why, why was she so mad at me, why was she leaving me, did those last few months really mean so little to her.

I suppose I could have just given up right now because she clearly didn't want to see me, but if I just let her leave like that, I knew I'd always regret it, maybe she'd be happy to see me, I shake my head as I climb in my car, Ethan had said she'd broken down in tears for hours, but I still didn't know why, it should have been me consoling her, but she wouldn't have let me, damn it, why was she so stubborn, why didn't she just tell me what I was supposed to have done wrong, so that I could fix it, she was clearly as miserable as I was and now she was running away, this was absolute insanity, but as I race down the motorway to try beat the clock, it doesn't matter if it's insanity, if I don't get to Laney on time, I may lose her forever—and that wasn't something I was willing to do.

As the seconds ticked by, every moment counted, I needed to get to that airport, I didn't have a plan, didn't people usually have a plan when they did something this impulsive, all I had was a passport, a credit card and a wish for a miracle.

Every second that ticks by my anxiety grows deeper, what if I'm too late, no, I can't think that, that's not even an option, but then again, what if I make it, then what, she doesn't want to see me, I can't see it being a happy reunion, my palms are sweaty, my heart is racing, I can feel the sweat pierce my brow, if I wasn't racing so fast to reach her I might start to have an anxiety attack. I don't have time for my body to have a meltdown, rolling down the window I feel the cold breeze instantly whip at my face, that feels much better, but as I look at the clock, shit, I'm running out of time, what if she's already boarded the plane, but I have to at least try, then if she ever came back she'd know, she'd know I tried to be there for her, she'd know I tried everything in my power to reach her.

I try call her phone but it goes straight to voicemail, can't say I'm shocked, she hasn't answered over the last couple of days, why would she answer now, for all I know, she's blocked my number and like an idiot I still repeatedly try, but that's what I would do, I'd try until my last dying breath because whether she knew it or not, she belonged with me.

The drive seems longer than it should do, after all, I'm manically thinking of all the things that could possibly go wrong, which makes my journey seem that much longer, it should have only been a 15 minute drive, it felt like I was on a never-ending road to hell, like running on a treadmill, no matter have fast you went, you still never got anywhere, finally I see the turning for the airport, shit, it looks busy, parking the car, I race to the first desk I see.

If this was a movie, there would be nobody there, I'd go to the front desk and get all the answers I wanted, everything would run in my favour, or she'd be sat there and I'd see her, our eyes would meet across the room—but this wasn't a movie, it appeared every man and his fucking dog was getting a flight, there's about ten people in front of me, shit, I scour the other lines and they're worse than the one I'm currently stood in.

After about an hour, I'm finally here, I've made it through the hellish line that seemed to go on forever, how hard was it to grab a ticket, why did they need to take so bloody long, striding up to the desk I'm greeted with a smile, I don't have time for mindless chit-chat I'm running out of time and I need them to work they're magic on that bloody keyboard that is currently the only thing between me and Laney, so I put on my best fake smile I can muster, hoping my charm will help me get to her, well it couldn't hurt right?

"I need to book a flight."

"Sure, where would you like to go?"

"That's the thing, I'm not sure."

"I don't think I'm following," she looks as confused as I feel, now I'd have to lie my way onto that plane.

"You see, my fiance—." I almost laugh at myself, Laney would sure get a kick out of this, "booked our tickets but I've left mine at home, so could you find out which flight it is by any chance?"

"I'm not sure—."

"I'd be ever so grateful, she can't fly alone, she has health issues."

"What kind of health issues?"

"As her doctor I'm not at liberty to give away her personal information—patient, doctor confidentiality, you understand." Handing my doctors badge to her hoping it will sweeten the deal, I hold my breath as she looks from me to the badge.

"Of course." She smiles. "Name?"

"Excuse me?"

"What is her name."

"Laney Powell." She simply nods as she goes back to typing, drumming my hands on the desk, I'm getting impatient, this might be the most scared I've ever been in my life, even more scary than getting on that bloody horse.

There's a few seats available, I'm in luck, hey maybe it is like the movies, or the universe is actually turning something in my favour, whatever the reason I'm grateful as I hand over my credit card and passport, she quickly hands the ticket and my belongings back into my hand.

"You might not make it on time." Damn universe!

"Flight 176 is taking off in 5 minutes, if you're quick you might just make it."

I don't stay for anymore idle chat, I simply thank her and leave, after all, I have to beat the clock, running down the terminal I eagerly search for where I need to be, zig-zagging in between the crowded bustle of bodies, running up the escalator and finally racing to terminal 10 c, I'm out of breath when I arrive, my heart is racing, my hands are clammy, the race here feels like I've run a marathon, but if I reach her in time it will all be worth it, just to see her big innocent eyes one more time, just to have her scent surround me, just to hear her sweet voice, just one more time, even if it's not the happy reunion that I hope it would be, just to see her one more time.

My heart is pounding almost out of my chest, I've never felt vulnerability the way I do right now, I'm so close, catching my breath I walk to the tiny desk. I'm about to see her, the flutters in the pit of my stomach almost make me feel sick, it feels like an eternity since I've seen her, my hope slowly diminishes as my eyes dart to the side of the desk, the doors are closing.

Oh,no.

I'm too late.

Twenty-Five

Fly Me Away

Sitting on the plane, I stare out of the window, awaiting for the plane to take off, was it impulsive, sure, but I needed space, I needed time to breathe, I needed to figure out my next steps, maybe flying to another country would give me the time I needed to think what I was going to do with the rest of my life. I couldn't think in that apartment, everywhere reminded me of him, I needed to go somewhere he hadn't been, yes, I was purging Beau from my system, well not really, he was a permanent fixture in my head, but if I could at least relax and stop the hurt for even a little while, a trip was a good thing, some women change their hair, some women worked out, me? It appeared I ran across the world to find myself, hey, whatever works right?

Now I was sat on the plane fear had kicked in, after all I'd never flown before, it was like sitting on a big bird that was more than likely going to crash mid-flight, shit, no, don't think about crashing, why did people even do this? My palms were already sweaty, my heart was racing, was that sweat dripping from my forehead.

I try regulate my breathing but the more I sit looking out of the window the more my breathing becomes erratic, why would I get on a plane, maybe I should just forget about my big adventure, yes, that sounded good, after all nobody but Alisa knew I was here, so I wouldn't need to explain anything, after all, was I really going to let Beau ruin the rest of my life. I hadn't resigned, so there was still time to continue my miserable life, but what if I'd miss out on something amazing, I want to get up, I want to get up and go back to my safe apartment where my palms don't sweat in terror, but my legs won't move. I'm rooted to the spot and all I can think is, *'oh-my-god, I'm going to die'* no, I couldn't die, I was having a baby, shit, was this irresponsible to my unborn child, I shake my head, no, what would be irresponsible to your child would be to bring a child into the world, mentally unstable, no, this trip would help me clear my head and if it didn't at least I could say I'd taken one adventure before the baby had arrived.

"Are you okay?"

"Is it that obvious." I smile, looking up at the flight attendant.

"Nervous flier?"

"First time."

"Would you like a drink, it usually takes the edge off."

"I can't, but I'd love some water." She nods as she turns and walks away.

Pulling down the shutter on the window, I think maybe, just maybe if I can't see the outside maybe I will forget that I will be plummeted fifty meters into the sky at any moment, it was the waiting that was the worst part, waiting to feel the vibrations beneath your feet, waiting for the oncoming panic attack that I could feel racing through my body, laying back I close my eyes, *deep breath in, hold for five, long breath out, deep breath in, long breath out, deep breath in, long breath out,* it seemed to be working, my heartbeat that had nearly burst out of my chest moments ago was now slowing to a normal rate, the blood was slowly moving through my body instead of rushing into my head, a sense of calmness overcomes my body, I feel lighter, more at peace.

"Hey, little star."

"I'm not speaking to you," I pout, how had he found me? The plane hadn't even taken off yet, but here he was, it was impossible, I didn't even know where we were going, so how did he?

"Come on, Laney, you know—."

"I don't want to hear it—leave."

"I'm sure you said that last time."

"Well, I mean it this time."

"You didn't mean it last time?"

"What, yes—no—I don't know." His hand crawls up my thigh, I feel the tingles instantly, it's not like before, it's instant, little goosebumps follow his fingers wherever he touches me, "please, Beau." I beg.

"You didn't think I'd let you leave me, did you." His lips are on my neck and my body melts into his touch, oh fuck, I'd missed him.

I should tell him no, I should tell him this isn't what I want, but this is everything I want, this is everything I've thought about for the last few days, hearing his voice, feeling his touch, just melting into his embrace once more, but I couldn't forgive him could I? No that wasn't even a question I couldn't forgive him, but he felt—so fucking good, I was moaning just from having his lips pressed against my sensitive neck.

"God, I've missed you." He breathes into my neck, I want to say it back so much, but his fingers are once again playing havoc with my body, shit, when did I become so sensitive, every touch is like a mini explosion erupting deep inside of my body, "didn't you miss me." I can't answer, his fingers are teasing my nipples through my sheer blouse, the material mixed with Beau's touch is causing my body to writhe with pleasure.

I can already feel the pooling between my legs, hard gasps fall from my lips, "oh, you did miss me." His fingers pull my hardened nipple harder, fuck, "you missed me touching you like this, if I reached down—." his hands move lower past my stomach, "I bet I'd find you soaking fucking wet." Dipping his hands into my sweat pants he moves his fingers up and down against my pussy causing me to writhe beneath his touch, spreading my legs wider, "oh, you fucking want my fat fingers inside your dripping pussy don't you." Once again he slides his fingers up and down, "if you want me to fuck you, you better give me an answer, or I could just tease you like this." His fingers once again move up and down my slimy wet pussy, lingering a little too long across my clit, I cry out once more, "say it," my breathing is rapid, my heart is beating fast, "say, I want you to fuck me," I try pushing my hips up, hoping that his fingers will accidentally slide inside, but he knows my game even before I get to thrust my hips, "say it Laney, tell me how badly you want me to fuck you, I need to hear you say it." He doesn't let up, his fingers tease me, but never slip inside, every touch, every slight movement, internally I'm screaming, this is pure torture, he encircles my clit with his thumb and I very nearly lose my mind, "please, Beau." I gasp, he's so close to my dripping hole. I can almost feel how full I know he'll make me once he slips inside, "please." I beg once more, "god, your so fucking wet, don't you want me to fill you up baby," I nod, "then—say—it, tell me to fuck you," I've never felt anything like it before, I'm so close to cumming, I just need him to push me over the edge, "oh fuck, please Beau, fuck me." I finally gasp.

"That's all you needed to say," he smiles, while ragging my sweat pants off of my legs, "what are you doing?" He unbuttons his jeans sliding them across his ass, picking me up he places me on his knee, "Beau—."

"Is that a trick question?" I shake my head, "I'm doing what you asked."

"But—."

"Did you not ask me to fuck you?"

"Yes, but—."

"Oh, you thought I wanted to fuck you with my fingers," he lets out a chuckle, "what did I tell you?" I stare at him blankly, "my cum belongs inside of you baby, always inside of you," I'm going to protest, after all we are on a fucking plane, I'm naked from the waist down and Beau has his fucking hardened cock bobbing up and down like it's getting ready to win a race. I'm about to climb off of him because this is absolute madness, allowing him to finger fuck me was bad enough but this was just crazy! I'm not sure why he thought I'd agree to this, I wasn't agreeing to this, on a plane full of people, this was worse than joining the mile high club.

Lifting my hips I try move my body away from his, his hands instantly grip my hips tighter, moving me closer, shit, closer? "Now, where do you think you're going." I shake my head, "Beau, we can't—." He raises my body into the air and in one swift movement brings my body down, as my body comes down, he moves his cock at my centre, pushing up, he slides in with ease, my back arches as I cry out at the sudden impact of his cock entering me, "whoops," he smiles, whoops, whoops, he'd just slammed my pussy hard against his cock and all he could say was whoops, that didn't seem like the right word, not right now, but oh fuck, he feels so fucking amazing. Every fiber in my body is screaming with pleasure, the way his cock massages my insides causes my body to set alight, I'm not even aware but my hips start thrusting taking his thick cock deeper, the cries erupt from my body like they've been begging to be released, "oh baby, you're on fucking fire," jumping up and down I bounce on his cock like I need to feel the hard thrust that my body gets with every jolt, "fuck, Laney, you feel so fucking nice, don't fucking stop," he cries, harder and faster, I feel him fill me up, his hands reach for my swollen breasts, massaging and pulling them as I move faster and faster on top of his cock, screams fill the air as I finally burst open the dam, spilling all of my pleasure all over his delicious thick cock, "I love you," he whispers into my hair.

Opening my eyes, my eyes dart across the plane looking around to see if we've been carted off for indecent exposure, but I'm alone, there's no cock beneath me, sweat pierces my body, my shirt is glued to my sticky, slick wet skin, my breathing is ragged. I'm breathless, shit, was it only a dream, what a fucking dream it was, of course it was a dream, he hadn't come here, I was still flying off for my great adventure, I hear the rumbling beneath my feet, we must be in the air now, why would I dream about him now, that dream was explicitly glorious, I can feel the excitement between my thighs.

"Damn it, Beau." I utter out loud.

"Yes, darling," looking to the seat next to me, my eyes finally meet his, there he is, Beau.

I had to be dreaming, yes, that was it, I was still dreaming, after all isn't this how the dream started before he fucked me into oblivion, my mind sure was cruel, creating a dream inside a dream, was that even possible, but looking at him now, he seemed very fucking real, maybe this wasn't a dream because he was looking at me with a rather confused look on his face, oh shit, had he heard me, did I talk in my sleep, or moan, I didn't know, but he had that same wicked grin on his face that he'd always wore when he was about to get his own way.

"Miss me." He smiles.

Twenty-Six

A Surprising Turn Of Events

He was just unbelievable, when I thought he couldn't stoop any lower, there he was looking like the cat who'd got the cream, smiling at the side of me, how had he found me? I didn't even know where this plane was heading, so how did he?

"Leave."

"We are in the air." He smirks.

"I don't care, just leave."

"Like, plummet to my death, would that make you happy, little star." His hand reaches out, I feel his fingertips lightly brush against my skin, whipping my head away from him I scowl.

"Beau—."

"You wouldn't speak to me—."

"So, you thought you'd high Jack my holiday."

"Is that what is—a holiday?"

"What else would it be."

"I don't know, seems to me like you're running away."

"Yeah, well I didn't run far enough because you're here, once again, why am I not surprised, you are the most selfish, obnoxious—." He pulls my head close to his, I try moving my head once more but I'm just not fast enough, his lips press against mine, for the slightest moment I melt into his touch, then I remember the heartache he's put me through and I pull away, "Laney—."

"No, this isn't fair, this isn't fair to me, haven't you done enough."

"Laney—."

"No, Beau, what do you fucking want from me."

"I don't want anything from you."

"Then why don't you fucking leave me alone." He grabs both sides of my head with his hands, I try to shake out of his grip but he holds me there firmly, "I can't leave you alone, don't you see."

Closing my eyes, "why." I utter.

"I've fucking fallen in love with you—okay, I love you Laney."

"Yeah, do you also love the blonde I saw in your office?"

"That's what this is about." He drops his hands, releasing my face.

"Of course that's what this is about." He looks at me with a strange look on his face, but then the strangest thing happens, his shocked face turns to a smile and now it was my turn to look confused, he then breaks into an out roar of laughter, "great Beau, I'm glad you find this funny."

"Oh, I do."

"You're an asshole."

"Yeah and you're stubborn."

"Why, because unlike your string of many other women—."

"What women Laney?"

"The one in your office—."

"Oh you mean—my sister."

"Your—."

"Yes, Laney, Mary-Anne is my sister, I'd have introduced you but you ran off in a hurry." My hands go over my eyes, I'm so embarrassed, I'd put myself through all this heartache and for what? For a misunderstanding.

"Why are you still here?"

"Shit, Laney I just told you—."

"No, I mean after the way I've treated you, why are you here." His face softens, he brings his hand across my cheek, but this time I let him, "I've loved you since I first laid eyes on you, in that library, I knew it was you from that very first day, you don't really think I'd let the only girl I gave my heart to a long time ago slip through my fingers do you."

"But I don't deserve you." I sob as fresh tears crawl down my face.

"Oh, little star, it's I that doesn't deserve you, but I'm hoping you see that we belong together, you see I fell for you a long time ago, but these last few months I fell hard and when you left, I lost something—." I'm breathless, "what did you lose?" I gasp, a small slip of a smile falls across his lips, "I lost my star."

He catches my face with his hand pressing his lips hard against mine, I finally let go, I surrender to his touch and once again allow his warmth to fill my heart, with one touch he lights me up from the inside, as his tongue flicks against mine I finally pour every part of myself into his touch and I finally get the sense of coming back home, laying back my fingers slide into his, feeling his warmth as his palm presses against mine, I smile.

"Laney, I have one more question."

"Yeah?"

"Where are we going?"

Gazing into his eyes, I smile, "I have no idea." Our mixed laughter fills the air, home is not a place, home is where you feel happiest, with Beau's hand wrapped against mine, this is the closest place to home I'd ever got, I used to dream of a family, now I had one, they were my home, closing my eyes, I finally find peace.

Twenty-Seven

Perfect

That plane ride was my greatest adventure, an adventure I'd thought I'd be taking alone—it seemed Beau had other ideas, he'd never gave up on me, even when I'd given up myself, he was always there, I just couldn't see it.

When we landed, we just stood there in awe, I wasn't sure what this holiday was supposed to be, maybe he was right, maybe I was running away, I was running away because I was falling, but he'd been there to catch me, the fresh ocean air had filled my nostrils, the air felt different or maybe I was just different because I'd given myself over to the fact I could no longer run from my own heart. I'd surrendered to him and he'd given me a strong hand and a heart full of love, it had been there all along, my fear had held me back from seeing what my brain wouldn't allow, I couldn't see him before but as he stood before me his feet mushed into the sand, carefree and happy, I had one more thing to do.

"Beau." He looks at me like I hold all the secrets to the universe in my eyes, "There is a reason I visited you that day."

"In my office?" I nod, "you were going to profess your undying love." He mocks.

"I'd already done that, I've got a secret," I whisper.

"Oh yeah?"

"Remember how you always said your cum—." He growls, "belongs inside of me always," a wicked smile appears on his lips, wrapping my arms around his neck, nuzzling my face into his neck, I lift my head, "I'm pregnant," I whisper.

His eyes widen, his smile instantly grows, the crystalline of his blue eyes starts twinkling, lifting me up by my waist, he twirls me around and around, while I giggle, bringing his face close to mine, "now, everything is perfect," he whispers into my mouth, before his lips crash against mine, with only the waves of the ocean filling my ears, I get lost in the magic that is Beau.

I came here to find myself, but I found something else entirely, I find a love that burned through my soul, I found a love that had long been waiting for me, I'd found Beau—finally I'd found Beau, I wasn't sure what life would be like now, but with Beau by my side, one thing was for sure, it would never be dull.

I'd avoided this man because I'd thought he would ruin me, I'd thought he'd break me into little pieces and I'd never be whole again, but he'd saved me, I'd found home.

I never thought that this was even possible, Beau, I'd always thought of as the ultimate ladies man, a fun time guy who wasn't looking for anything, while I was busy scowling at what I'd assumed was his many string of women, he was busy looking at me, I was completely oblivious to what was standing in front of me the whole time, this Christmas I'd been given a gift I didn't even know I needed, I'd been given the gift of sight, you see I'd been blind this entire time, searching for a love that would with stand the test of time, he'd waited for me for five years and I never even saw it. I didn't think it was possible for anyone to love me as ferociously as Beau had, maybe I didn't think I deserved it, or maybe it's because I'd never been loved, but he was here, he'd raced to reach me just in time because sometimes—just sometimes we run from the feelings that scare us the most, but maybe that's when we need to jump with blind faith, maybe we just need to trust that when we jump he will be down there with his arms open wide waiting to catch you.

I'd thought I was lost, I'd thought I was invisible, maybe when we are searching in the dark, blind and we lost, all we really want is to be found, Beau had found me a long time ago, I was just too blind to see him, but as I look at him now, I see him, I see all of him.

"Now everything is perfect." He smiles.

"Even if I open my mouth," I wink.

"Well you know—he moves his head close to mine, his breath sending shivers across my body as his warm breath hits my skin, "there are ways to make you shut up."

"Is that a promise," I bite my lip in anticipation, as he holds my body close to his, feeling him envelope me within his warm embrace, I'd never envisioned what perfect would look like but I'm sure it felt something—like this.

"Come on little star," he smiles.

“where are we going?”

“Home.”

Impossible I think, while staring into his eyes, I was already home, Beau was my home, home was no longer a place, wherever Beau was, that was my home, he’d healed every trauma I’d ever had in my life and wrapped in his loving embrace, he’d not only opened my heart, but he’d made my soul dance, perfect wasn’t the standard we were told it was, perfect was finding someone perfectly imperfect made for you—your own version of perfect.

Walking down the beach with his hand firmly clasped in mine, a warmth spreads through my body as I whisper into the night sky,

“Perfect.”

About Author

Lilura Sloane is predominately a provocative romance writer, Lilura wanted her readers to fall in love with the idea of being in love because isn't love the most magical thing you can possess, we all search for it, but some of us never find it.

Lilura also writes under another pen name, she wanted to break down her genres, so she also writes under Skye Hale as Lilura Sloane has been marketed as a romance writer, Sky Hale writes all things thriller, mystery, horror, Lilura always loved this genre.

Lilura was born and raised in the United Kingdom, she currently resides here with her five children, who for the most part drive her up the wall (haha) but are very supportive of her writing.

Lilura's writing journey started when an accident at work left her with a chronic illness, unable to work, she found a love of writing and creating characters, new worlds and new possibilities.

You can follow Lilura here:

tiktok.com/lilurasloane

instagram.com/authorlilurasloane

facebook.com/Lilurasloane

goodreads.com/LiluraSloane

bookbub.com/LiluraSloane

Visit my website:

https://www.lilurasloanebooks.com

Want book release updates:

https://books2read.com/author/lilura-sloane/subscribe/1/296452/

Grab a free book when you subscribe to my mailing list:

https://storyoriginapp.com/giveaways/74b92c0a-531d-11ed-a724-db5ddd4eb4cc

https://storyoriginapp.com/giveaways/b0dd0c76-523f-11ed-9ab2-d39767ae7800

https://storyoriginapp.com/giveaways/e88dd2a4-5221-11ed-98a8-470ea93cec07

https://storyoriginapp.com/giveaways/ae9a4df6-5150-11ed-8028-579d4f46d2f7

Also By LILURA

A chance encounter between a mysterious neighbour and the shy girl next door could be the perfect element of excitement and danger - or a delicious disaster in the making - in Lilura Sloane's Wicked desires series...

I am the type of woman who plays it safe. In my personal life working at the publishing house - i like safe, i like control and i like comfort but i'm in my twenties and I've never been kissed-yes i know tragic! So I'm dipping my feet into the dating pool, so far I'm not impressed, i should just give it up as a bad job - that is until i meet - him.

Ryker Jones is as sexy as sin, and I've developed some weird obsession to him, from the moment i moved next door to my mysterious neighbour, which has led me to do the most impulsive thing I've ever done in my life. Maybe it was his hero act when he saved me from that slime ball who didn't take no for an answer, or maybe it was just him. I had my first kiss - but it wasn't just any kiss - it - was - a panty melting - leg shaking - rock my world kind of kiss. Goodbye sanity - hello madness.

A forbidden love story about fate, heartache, and second chances.

She was forbidden A line i was never going to cross.

Davina is sweet, tempting—she reminds me of Kala—that's not why i want her, no, i'm sure it's not that. She's twenty-one, she sexy as sin, but she's my best friend's daughter.

But like all gut-wrenching situations, my past and future collide in a cruel twist of fate.

My tortured past will test the bounds of my sanity, nothing will ever be the same again.

Redemption, will cost me everything...

We must find the essence of been in love.

When her childhood crush invites her to Paris Skye runs with her heart instead of her head. Her brother is in a jam and needs help—but what's new. Daniel Valencia is her brothers best friend and her lifetime crush.

Running off to Paris is reckless, she knows this, but if she doesn't go she'll always wonder...

Meet me in a Paris.

Those simple words gave her a chance to find herself. In the process she'd find something she never expected.

A heart wrenching, tortured hero romance, featuring a broken man in need of redemption and an innocent, lively heroine who sees through the madness.

He was lost when i found him...

Alex has been a friend of the family since before i was born, we've never really spent much time together, the odd email, the odd letter, the lavish gifts... that was until i was invited to go stay with him for four years while i attend university.

Penelope was a sweet thing, Alex's third marriage was falling apart- he knew why his wife stayed...the money, he was apathic over his situation, buried his head in work...that was until she showed up... Penelope knew she must be crazy to fall for a man whose heart was broken. It was risky- but it was a risk she was willing to take.

She knew it could end in her heartbreak but when you find something this precious in the dark, it's only natural to want to bring it out into the light....

One night at the bewitching Jewel.

That's all it took.

One glance stole my breath, One-touch lit me on fire.

Our chemistry was undeniable And erasing Hunter from my mind is impossible.

Our connection is still as strong as the night we met, but he's ignoring me, he's acting like we've never met. Of course, I know why, the air feels thicker whenever I'm near him, so there's only one thing I can do, pretend we never met and erase that night from my memory, ignore my new professor.

The night we met I was broken and he made me whole again.

I didn't know how I could erase that night from my memory, But I also didn't know if I'd be able to stay away from him...

Afterword

Hello, reader.

And here we are. You and me on the last page.

Don't search for love, be like Laney, let love find you.

Maybe you already have a Beau and just like Laney you just can't see that he's always been there loving you, supporting you, waiting for you, we often don't see what is right in front of us, maybe you don't have a Beau, but maybe you will, you cannot force love, love is patient, love is kind, love will make you slowly lose your mind. Laney and Beau's story, while a work of fiction, is a belief in not just finding **'the one'** it's also about learning to love yourself, heal from your trauma, learn to be carefree, learn to get in touch with that inner child, be that girl with fairy dust in her hair, dreams bigger than the ocean, dance, be silly, when you are not looking at anyone but yourself, you'd be surprised who has been looking for you and looking at you all along.

Love comes in many shapes and forms, if you do one thing today, make yourself a promise.

Promise to love yourself a little more each day.

You will see just how important you are in this big world full of possibilities.

You're magic baby!

You just need to look.

All my love always,

Lilura Sloane xoxo

Printed in Great Britain
by Amazon

29194327R00131